Without Tess

MARCELLA PIXLEY

SQUARE
FISH

FARRAR STRAUS GIROUX
NEW YORK

SQUARE FISH

An Imprint of Macmillan
175 Fifth Avenue
New York, NY 10010
macteenbooks.com

Square Fish books may be purchased for business or promotional use. For
information on bulk purchases, please contact the Macmillan Corporate and
Premium Sales Department at (800) 221-7945 x5442 or by e-mail at
specialmarkets@macmillan.com.

Library of Congress Cataloging-in-Publication Data
Pixley, Marcella Fleischman.
    Without Tess / Marcella Pixley.
      p.   cm.
    Summary: Fifteen-year-old Lizzie Cohen recalls what it was like growing up
with her imaginative but disturbed older sister Tess, and how she is striving to
reclaim her own life since Tess died.
    ISBN 978-1-250-04435-8 (paperback) / 978-1-4299-6982-6 (ebook)
    [1. Sisters—Fiction.   2. Guilt—Fiction.   3. Death—Fiction.
4. Emotional problems—Fiction.   5. Mental illness—Fiction.   6. Jews—United
States—Fiction.]   I. Title.

PZ7.P68947Wi 2011   [Fic]—dc22   2011001469

Originally published in the United States by Farrar Straus Giroux
First Square Fish Edition: 2014
Book designed by Alexander Garkusha
Square Fish logo designed by Filomena Tuosto

10   9   8   7   6   5   4   3   2   1

AR: 4.6 / LEXILE: 790L

For Dorothy and Sidney Sokol
and
for Jill

I know I never said goodbye
I couldn't bear to see you cry

S—

It looks lame, but it's actually pretty good. I cried... but you know me.

warning: makes you want to jump off a clif

—W

FUNERAL LILIES

Every Wednesday I bring the battered Pegasus Journal into the high school guidance office. I sit in the rocking chair and lean back so it feels as if the world is holding its breath. I've grown to like this room. I like the painted masks, each one with its own hollow eyes. I like the wooden animals on the bookshelf: the camel, the stork, the wolf raising her face to the moon; but my favorite of all is the wooden horse that hangs from strings above my head. Its mane and tail are made of real hair, and it has red glass mirrors for eyes. It looks into the distance, its dusty head crooked. Tess would have loved this horse. She would have tried to convince me its eyes could cast a spell. I might have believed her when I was a little girl, but now I know better. There's no such thing as magic. *I'll never let you go, Lizzie. No matter what happens to me, I'll never ever let you go.*

I always come five minutes early. I like to sit in the rocking chair and breathe away everything real. Bad grades and teachers who frown when they see me. Letters sent home in sealed envelopes. All the kids who give me distance like I'm some kind of human plague walking the hallway. I breathe away the silence of Isabella Amodeo, who has pitied me for almost five years and who continues to pity me, no matter how much time goes by. That first week, she delivered casseroles to our doorstep: warm food drowned in melted cheese and tomato sauce, meals Mamma could place on the table without looking. I remember sitting down to dinner, staring at the empty chair.

Of course, there were other kindnesses too. Floral arrangements delivered to the door from our teachers, bouquets of white funeral lilies so pungent they made me cross-eyed. I smelled nothing but funeral lilies that whole first month. Even outside the house—even when I was able to get away from the parade of relatives and neighbors, people who would look at me with sad eyes and then turn away—the smell of funeral lilies clung to my skin, my hair, my clothes. The scent was so strong I still smell it sometimes when I think about how it felt to be without her for the first time. So that now, sadness still smells like funeral lilies to me, and strangely, so does the feeling of loneliness, and so does the feeling of relief, because those were all things that I had never known before Tess left me just Lizzie all alone.

Dr. Kaplan walks into the office at 12:35 and sits at his desk. "Okay, kiddo," he says, "just give me a second." He finds my file and mumble-reads his notes from our last session. Then he settles back into his chair and waits for me to open Tess's battered Pegasus Journal.

The whole thing with the Pegasus Journal was his idea. At our very first session, I told him about the journal filled with sketches and poems. I told him how I rescued it from her coffin the day of her funeral and carried it home in the inside pocket of my coat, how I couldn't let them bury it, because I knew that these pages contained the real story of Tess and me and what happened when things changed. Even though I might not want to remember, burying the Pegasus Journal along with Tess would have been criminal. On that first Wednesday, he told me we had no choice. We had to use the Pegasus Journal to help me come to terms with what happened.

"Ready when you are," Kaplan says, smiling.

It's time to start. I open the Pegasus Journal. The pages are fragile, dog-eared, smudged with fingerprints and shadows. Here is a girl with worms in her hand. Here is an army of toads. Here is the profile of a drowning horse. But it is Tess's face that gazes back at me. Tess's eyes and wild red hair. I catch my breath. I remember the day she drew this. How she rubbed in shadows that made the cheek seem three-dimensional, the ears perfectly lobed like funeral lilies. How she used the back of her thumb to bring out the light in each eye so it looked as though the horse was gazing off into the distance somewhere, at a world unraveling, its tangled mane whipping around its face like the tangled hair of a wild girl who doesn't even care enough to comb a hand through the snarls. The horse on the page opens its mouth. It is my sister's voice coming up through the years. *I'll never let you go, Lizzie. No matter what happens to me, I'll never ever let you go.*

FLYING HORSES

Milk-white steeds with flashing hooves
Canter 'cross the boathouse roofs
Through the tides that flash with foam
Merlin bring my horses home.

Feathered wings and golden tail
Flashing eyes and silken sail
Canter brave through crashing waves
Far above the drowned men's graves.

FLYING HORSES

"What kind of wings do you want?"

Tess raises one eyebrow and waits for me to talk. I don't answer right away. She is eleven and I am nine. It is one week before summer vacation. This is a big decision because whatever wings I choose will be on my back for the rest of my life. We are sitting Indian-style beneath our dining room table, surrounded by the familiar legs of Mamma's writing group, the ragtag bunch of grownups who come to our house once a month on a Saturday with their pages and their pens, to drink iced tea, and talk and cry. Here are Mamma's skinny legs with her embroidered sandals. Here are the poet's straight, uncomfortable legs with her high-heeled black boots. Here are the mystery writer's sickly legs covered with scabs and sores. Here are the picture-book writer's old-lady legs, puffy and swollen, with her blue spiderweb veins, and her red potato feet powdered and pushed into loafers.

Tess and I always spend these meetings sitting under the table making plans for our escape. Tess is holding the Pegasus Journal. She has drawn six different sets of wings, each on its own page. Each set of wings costs seventy-five-thousand dollars and fifty-nine cents, but that's okay because Tess is royalty and she keeps real silver coins hidden under her pillow. There are wings made of the following magical substances: water, gumdrops, moonbeams, gold dust, magic feathers, and peanut butter. Only stupid horses choose peanut butter. Peanut butter wings are gooey. They melt in the sun. The stupid horses who choose peanut butter try to fly, but they always fail. They start off just like Merlin taught us—take a running start and then leap up into the sky. *Fly fly, high high, up in the sky, up in the sky.* But the stupid horses end up falling flat on their faces. *Ker-splatt.* Talented horses choose moonbeams or feathers brushed with gold dust. Tess tells me I am one of the most promising horses in our class, and I know this must be true because Merlin tells her everything. Tess taps on the Pegasus Journal and looks down her nose at me. She makes a *tick tock tick tock* noise with her tongue to tell me that time is running out.

"I'll have gold-dust feathers," I tell her finally, finding the right page. "I'm a black horse. My mane and tail are gold and I have a gold streak down my nose." I pet my nose with one finger.

Tess pats my bangs, scratches me behind one ear, and picks up a gold Magic Marker. With one thin hand, she holds my face still. With the other, she draws a line down the bridge of my nose. The Magic Marker feels cool and wet like a tongue.

"Do you have a star or a diamond?"

"A diamond," I tell her, showing her the shape with my fingers. "And I have one gold stocking. On my left front leg. When I trot you can see it flashing and when I canter it's like a golden blur. That's why they call me Sun Dancer."

"Nice to meet you, Sun Dancer." Tess bows her head and I bow back. She colors a gold diamond on my forehead and a gold band around my left wrist. Even though her fingers are skinny-skinny like baby fingers, they are sharp. They dig into my skin and make me want to pull away. Tess puts her elbow down on my arm until I keep it still. "This'll look cool with the gold wings," she assures me. "Merlin thinks you made a good choice. He says he's glad you've come to study with us."

"When will the magic be complete?"

Tess leans forward so she can whisper into my ear. "In about ten minutes," she says. Her breath is too warm on my cheek. The closeness makes me dizzy. "That's when you'll become a Pegasus. I'll get my moonbeam wings a little earlier since I'm older. I'm black with a gray blaze and a gray muzzle. That's why they call me Smoke. I have magical powers. I can see into the future. Plus I can move objects with my mind. Those are powers Merlin taught me. Here. Draw my markings."

Tess closes her eyes and her face gets still and expectant. I take the gray Magic Marker and color a gray stripe down her forehead. Then I color a circle around her nose and mouth. One of the writers says something muffled and the rest of them laugh. There is the sound of chairs shifting, and people shuffling manuscripts. Ice cubes and glasses clinking. "I don't think Mamma's going to like this," I tell her. "She thinks we're playing tic-tac-toe." We look around us at all the grownups' legs. The mystery writer leans forward and scratches a sore underneath her knee. Then she folds her napkin across her lap and smooths out her skirt with the wrinkled palms of her hands. "I don't want to get in trouble. Mamma doesn't like it when we interrupt the group."

Tess grins. "You still don't understand, do you? They don't need to know everything. Besides"—she brings her face even closer to mine—"we're immortal. We don't need parents. Merlin's in charge of us now. Make my muzzle darker. I think you missed a spot. And make sure my blaze is sort of like a triangle." Tess turns to a new page in the Pegasus Journal. Quick as a flash, she scribble-sketches a horse's head. The mane is blowing in the wind and all the different locks are detailed with lines and shadows so you can really imagine the animal staring off into the distance with its fierce, magical eyes shining. Tess colors in the pupil with the edge of her pencil and leaves a white highlight so it looks like the eye is real. Tess hands over the Pegasus Journal and points at the horse that she wants to be.

"You're so good," I say, sighing, tracing the lines of the face with the edge of my pinkie finger. "I wish I could do that."

Tess shrugs and lifts her chin. "Make me a horse," she commands. I darken my lines. I keep the color inside the circle a solid gray. I trace the contours of her mouth without touching the insides of her lips at all. I work slowly until the job is done. Tess keeps her eyes closed. Then she sways a little. She sticks out her tongue and starts making wet, strangled noises like she's going to throw up.

"What's wrong?" I ask.

"The magic," Tess croaks. "The wings. It's happening. It *hurts*." She rolls herself into a ball. She moves her shoulder blades up and down, wincing and clutching at herself. I can almost see the moonbeam wings coming up from the surface of her back, pushing through the skin, the long, white bones rising like glaciers from the sea, the moonbeams feathering out, each tiny filament, shining, sparkling, until she has wings, beautiful, new, magnificent wings. Tess hunches her back. Then she uncurls, tosses her neck, and whinnies. She turns from one profile to the next, admiring her brand-new moonbeam wings. They are even more special and more magical than Merlin said they would be.

"They are incredible," I breathe.

"I know they're incredible. I can feel them on my back. Lizzie, I need to fly. You've got to get me out of here. If I stay under this table another minute I'll die." Her eyes fill with tears and she begins to shake like the time she had that high fever and Mamma had to put her in a bathtub filled with ice.

"But if we go out, they'll see you."

"Merlin taught me how to turn us invisible." Tess begins to wave her hands in the air.

I grab her skinny wrists. "I think we should stay here until after they're all done with their meeting. If Mamma sees us, she'll make us wash off the Magic Marker. We'll get in trouble."

Tess looks at me, hurt, like I've betrayed her. "It's not Magic Marker," she insists. "I keep telling you. It's magic paint. It's changed me. I'm a Pegasus now. Look at my wings. There's nothing the grownups can do to change me back. After all of your training, after all of your flying lessons, you've got to believe me."

I look at her. She is my sister. She has Mamma's eyes and Daddy's chin and she has gray Magic Marker all over her face. She doesn't have wings growing out of her back. She just has a skinny spine like she's had since I can remember, and shoulder blades that are too sharp for a girl. I look and look at her but I don't see anything. I blink my eyes.

"Don't you believe me, Lizard?" Her eyes are wide. The familiar nickname tugs on my heart and makes me reach out for her. She twines her fingers into mine and looks into my face like she is looking into a mirror.

"Of course I believe you," I mutter.

Tess exhales. I exhale too.

"Let's go," she whispers.

And then I am pulling her out from under the table. We duck between the mystery writer and the poet and we run like our lives depend on it, past the scraggly writers who are drinking their iced tea and looking at their pages over half spectacles and don't see the two invisible horses galloping in bathing suits through the living room, one black with a golden blaze and a golden stocking, the other the color of smoke, with moonbeam wings extending from her shoulders as if she were an angel. They don't see us leap over the coffee table. We link arms and canter together, *one two three, one two three, one two three,* lifting our knees in unison, through the green double screen doors and out onto the long, wooden wraparound porch overlooking the pine needle hill and the tidal river that leads to the nearby ocean. We go down the porch stairs to the hill and take a running start, and then just as I leap with her, my own wings come, my beautiful gold-dust feathers extending from my shoulder blades like sunlight spreading out across the horizon, like beautiful beams of light. It doesn't hurt like Tess said it would. It feels like heaven. We are angels. I will never doubt her again. This is what it means to be immortal. Tess winks at me. She tosses her head and whinnies.

"Don't fly too close to the sun," Tess calls. "You'll burn the tips of your wings. Stay right with me. I'll keep you safe."

I gallop closer, but she bounds away, arching her neck and blowing air through her lips. She paws the air with cupped hands. She does cartwheels and somersaults and figure eights with her arms extended like wings. I'm getting out of breath trying to keep up. The sun beats down on our shoulders. Everything tastes like salt and sweat. The writers have moved outside to the porch. Mamma pours glasses of ice water. One at a time, the writers wander to the railing. They look down the hill at the river. I can hear the cool sound of ice against glass.

"I want a drink," I tell Tess.

"Drink some clouds." Tess stops and scoops pine needles into her hands and brings them to my face. I lower my muzzle and pretend to drink, but pine needles are nothing like fresh ice water, and I'm still thirsty.

Tess pulls me to her side and we link arms. *One two three. One two three. One two. One two.* We raise our knees like Irish dancers and toss our heads. If I watch Tess's doorknob knees from the corner of my eye, we can trot in time. When you trot, your breath bounces out of your mouth. *One two. One two. Knees and breath. Up and down. Huff huff. Huff huff.* Our bare feet slam the ground. The sun shines down. We trot and trot until we are both glazed with sweat and mosquitoes are buzzing around our heads. I wish I had a nice long horse's tail to swat them away.

Tess looks at me and grins. "Come on," she says.

"Where?"

"It's time for the splash landing. Then you can drink all you want."

Tess pulls us down the pine needle hill, over rocks and roots, across the cracked road, and down the rocky path to the shore. We trot in single file across the stationary dock, across the wooden ramp, and then onto the floating dock that rises and falls with the tide. We stand on the edge and breathe salt and wind. Mamma and the writers are lost in the distance a thousand miles behind us.

"Do you know what this is, Sun Dancer?" Tess asks me, swinging her arm in a wide arc.

"It's the floating dock," I say, smiling.

"No," Tess tells me, her voice soft and mysterious. "This is a huge, fluffy cumulus cloud over the river." She trickles her hands across invisible lumps and bumps, gathering invisible water and cupping her hands to her mouth to drink. I do the same. This time, when I finish drinking I feel quenched.

"Look down at the river."

I do. The sun winks off the water. The wind makes ripples in the air and our cloud floats on the current. I spread my wings to keep my balance. The water is green and deep and the wind makes us cool. I close my eyes. Everything smells like sun and salt.

Tess begins to sing a spell in her magical language. It sounds a little like Hebrew, a little like Spanish, and a little like Korean. It is the language of winged horses.

Achem moon poon yung jung bo
Nardo pardo don lem syo
Caballero moon poon cho
Pinto minto song sing so.

"Are you ready to land, my magical sister?" Her voice is gentle.

"I'm ready."

"Don't be scared," says Tess. "Say *nardo pardo.*"

"*Nardo pardo!*" I screech.

Tess grabs my hand and we balance together at the edge of the float. We each have one wing out and we bend our knees. *One. Two. Three.* We leap together and splash, letting the river close over our heads. We smile at each other through the green haze, bubbles rising from our mouths. Tess can stay underwater longer than me. She holds her breath by puffing her cheeks and making her body slow.

It's easy but then it gets harder.

The first thing that happens is you can feel a special pressure in your ears and your eyes. It's bearable. You won't get anxious for another seven seconds or so, but you feel the difference. Then you start to feel a weight on your chest and neck, like someone is piling on rocks. A light-headed feeling. A fuzziness. Then the world starts to ring. You keep yourself still and slow, moving your hands, just barely, to keep from floating to the top. This is when I usually give up.

But Tess has a real gift. She stays down until it is almost too late.

I rise from the water and gasp the beautiful, beautiful air into my lungs.

Tess is still at the bottom. Her eyes are closed. Her red hair swirls like seaweed. I count the seconds. *One one thousand, two one thousand, three one thousand,* before she rises from the river and is my sister again.

CRAB CARCASS BINGO

Come hither, my dear one
And sit on the dock.
I'll sing you a song
Of a carcass licked clean
By the wind's pointy tongue
Or the tick of a clock
The pleasure of meat
Turning crusty and green.

CRAB CARCASS BINGO

If you want to play with crabs, you have to decide if you want them alive or dead. Live crabs scuttle under rocks and seaweed or dig themselves into mud, or they pinch the palm of your hand so that you screech and drop them back into the water, which is where they want to be anyway. If you get three or four live crabs in a bucket and shake them up, they'll fight. The big ones tease the little ones with their superhero claws flexing and their beady eyes rolling as if they were lunatic madmen. Tess likes to bother them by sticking her fingers into the pail. She strokes the tips of their pincers so they want to attack so badly their eyeballs bubble. It's not easy to find live crabs. You have to get down on your knees, turn over rocks and shards of old clay sewer pipes, and wait until the mud settles. But if you are quiet for long enough, they appear, like giant spiders scuttling sideways.

It's easier to find crabs when they are already dead: the babies that toddled away too long and got caught in dry reeds, the teenagers who went exploring and got stranded high up on rocks and dried out in the sun, one claw open. Crabs are beautiful when they die no matter how old they are. Their shells turn orange and dry as reeds. Dead crabs are more fun to play with than live crabs. You can make them do whatever you want. Dead crabs are like tiny puppets. You can pose them. You can stack them on top of each other. You can play school, or doctor, or army with them, lining them up in rows, giving them voices, making them tell knock-knock jokes. But the very best thing to do with dead crabs is play Crab Carcass Bingo. On the first day of summer vacation, Tess and I celebrate our freedom with a really rousing game. Crab Carcass Bingo is the most disgusting game Tess has ever invented, and it doesn't even cost two cents.

You don't need a bingo card or a checkerboard. Instead, you use the lines on the dock planks to set them up, biggest to smallest, in eight even rows, with the big ones in the back and the small ones in the front. I like the babies best, small and round as pennies. Tess likes the mamma crabs with plump blue claws. She gives them funny names like Garfinkle and Porpinplopper, and she makes them talk in gravelly voices. The last thing you absolutely must do before you can sit down to play Crab Carcass Bingo is locate a perfect crusher rock, rough and heavy, to be dropped on the bodies from above. Once you find your crusher rock, you can start the game.

Tess always goes first because she is older. She holds her crusher rock above the bodies and counts. *One, two, three, bingo.* Then she throws the rock down. The driest bodies crush best. Their brittle shells crunch into cornflakes. The wetter the body, the smaller the crunch. Wet bodies flatten like deflated balloons. Not very satisfying. The crunchiest ones are Tess's huge, dry mamma crabs, because these are the bodies that sometimes have bits of meat still inside them, and when they explode they smell like tacos. I love tacos.

We are facing each other, sitting cross-legged on the floating dock with our crabs lined up in eight even rows. Tess is winning as usual. You get twenty points for the big ones, ten for the medium ones, and five points each for the teeny-weenies. Tess has a strategy that works like magic and it probably is. She whips her hand down so her wrist snaps and the crusher bounces twice. Usually she gets whatever crab she's going for, plus a few others.

"Your turn," says Tess.

I take my crusher and whip it down. I demolish three teeny-weenies and a medium one. I laugh like a maniac. Soon the dock is covered in crab cornflakes, and every once in a while, I get up on my hands and knees and blow the pieces into the water. All around the dock, there is a floating parade of legs and pincers and backs moving out to sea.

"Lizzie," says Tess. "You're my best friend." She leans forward and kisses me on the top of my head.

I pick up a crab and make it talk in a chipmunk voice. "I love you, Mingus Mopey."

"Promise me."

I move the legs and make it promise. "Cross my heart. Hope to die. Stick a Froot Loop in my eye."

Tess frowns. "Jews aren't supposed to do that."

"I'm not crossing my heart, I'm crossing Lola's."

Tess grabs my wrist. "No," she says. Her voice is low and serious. "Any kind of crossing is bad luck unless you're Christian. If you cross Lola's heart, Merlin will hunt you down and kill you in your sleep."

"That would be bad," I say, giggling.

"Find another way to prove you love me."

I stare at her. Her eyes are wide and shining. "What do you want me to do?" I ask.

"I want you to eat her."

"What?"

"I want you to eat Lola."

Tess gestures to the dried-up crab in the palm of my hand.

"Put her in your mouth. Chew her thirty-six times and swallow. Then we'll be best friends forever. If you really love me you'll do it."

I put the body up to my nose and sniff. Taco.

"Okay," I say. "I will eat Lola."

"I'll say one two three bingo, and then you eat."

My heart is beating fast. Tess puts her hands on my knees.

She says, "One, two, three, bingo!" I close my eyes and push Lola into my mouth. I chew thirty-six times, just like Tess told me. Here's what I discover. Lola does not taste like a taco. She tastes like stinky feet. But I keep chewing. The pincers are the hardest part. They poke my tongue, and I have to crunch on them until they are small enough to go down. Every once in a while, I get a piece of dried meat. My stomach lurches but I keep on chewing. Thirty-four, thirty-five, thirty-six. Done.

I let out an enormous burp.

Tess shrieks with joy and pounds me on my back.

I gag and puke Lola all over the floating dock. Then I puke up everything I've eaten for the past two days. Hot dogs and rice and carrots and scrambled eggs and spaghetti. Then apple juice.

Tess wipes my mouth with the sleeve of her T-shirt.

"Poor Lizzie," she says. "Merlin must want you to keep kosher. He's punishing you. Crabs scuttle on the bottom of the ocean with all the fish poop. I forgot to tell you. They are completely forbidden. You should have known that. You failed the test, Lizzie."

I spit.

Tess pets my cheek. "You'd better start praying, Lizzie. Pray a magic spell to Merlin."

I stare at her.

"Face east so he can hear you."

She grabs me by the shoulders and turns me toward the sun.

"Say *Baruch atah Adonai eloheinu melech ha'olam*. I am sorry I ate a crab. I am a bad Jew and I will never do it again."

My stomach lurches. My insides sound like a burbling volcano.

"I am a bad Jew," I whisper.

"Ask him to forgive you."

"I am so sorry, Merlin. I am so sorry."

"That's right," says Tess. "Good girl."

Isabella at the
Water Fountain

It is almost fourth period. Students rush through the hallways clutching piles of books, shouldering backpacks, laughing. Isabella stands at the water fountain. She looks lovely when she drinks. She keeps her legs straight and bends at the waist, holding her hair and letting the water splash on her lips. When she rises, her friends gather. For a moment I can't see her through the crowd that laughs and links arms, a hive of blue jeans and binders. They shift from one hip to the other. Someone tells a joke, and Isabella laughs, a sound as sudden as wind chimes. I'm a different kind of girl. It isn't just the way I look—although I'm sure she wouldn't be caught dead with black combat boots or studded gloves. It's not just our grades or our taste in music. It's not even because she wears a tiny silver cross around her neck and I wear a dog's choke collar.

I'm different because of the secret I keep. I'm different

because I'm guilty, and unlike Isabella, I don't believe in confession. I don't take the body or the blood of the savior into my mouth once a week and I haven't said a prayer in five years. My sins will hang around my neck for as long as I live. And when it's time for me to leave this earth, I am fairly certain that I won't be seeing Isabella or anyone else in her family where I'm going. I'll be shaking hands with an entirely different gatekeeper.

When Isabella notices me, she looks away at first, just as she always does. Then she squares her pretty shoulders and forces herself to meet my eyes. It's just a moment. Contact. And then she goes distant. There's no need to speak. I know what she's thinking. *I'm so sorry, Lizzie. So, so sorry.* The same unspoken words every time I pass her in the hall, or when I saunter in late to Mr. Fabiano's algebra class, where I sit in the back with my boots on the seat and she sits in the front with the other good students who do their homework every night, who smile and look beautiful together, like a bouquet of colorful flowers all bending their heads over their graphing calculators, talking only loud enough to check their answers or explain a proof or clarify an equation.

Isabella puts one hand through her long, black hair. The silver cross gleams in the hollow of her throat. It's the same cross she wore to Tess's funeral five years ago. She glances at me again and I bug my eyes out and cough, staggering into the lockers. I cross myself with exaggerated gestures, and pull my choke collar tight like I'm strangling myself. Then I give her the finger. Isabella turns back to her beautiful friends and I stagger past her to the guidance office where I know Kaplan is waiting for me.

It wasn't my idea to go into therapy with Kaplan. It was part of the deal the guidance office made with my parents at the end of my freshman year when it became clear that I was not going to survive high school unless I got some serious help. It wasn't so hard to hold it together in elementary and middle school. Teachers have always been impressed with my robust vocabulary and my penchant for sarcasm. So what if she occasionally forgets to hand in her homework? This child is brilliant. Give her an A. But high school is different. In high school, when you don't keep up with your work, it catches up with you—until you are buried under it like an overwhelmed little corpse. Until they find you crouched in the corner of the girls' bathroom with a broken pen, making red scratches down your arm because something about that kind of pain feels manageable, that kind of pain makes sense, the blood rising to the surface like a sunrise.

If I had been any other kid, they would have sent me to the nurse for a Band-Aid. A phone call home. A few weeks with a guidance counselor. Maybe summer school. But, oh my goodness, look at her file. This Lizzie Cohen is special, dang nabbit. When someone like Lizzie Cohen goes off the deep end, she doesn't get a guidance counselor, she gets

Dr. Kaplan, Ph.-bloody-D., because this is serious, folks. This girl has suffered a trauma, and we educators and administrators must mobilize our forces and make sure she has just what she needs to succeed. Maybe, just maybe, she is getting tired of walking around pretending to be strong for all of us. Maybe, just maybe, she is getting tired of convincing us that she is happy and well adjusted. Maybe, ladies and gentlemen, this is a cry for help.

So now they give me countless lectures about how important it is to turn myself around, how most colleges won't even consider a kid with Ds on her transcript even if she does read Faulkner and James Joyce in her free time. Teachers love to give me reminders about my appearance and my attitude. It's true. I have let my looks go since I started high school. And I suppose I tend to blend in with the alternative kids in this school, goth chicks who wear black eyeliner, who lean against the gymnasium during free periods to smoke or sketch, who saunter into class after the late-bell rings, who sass the teacher, who sit in the back row doodling graffiti tags on their desks with fine-point pens.

According to Principal Palazzola, who checks in with me every few weeks to see if I'm on the right track, I have more going for me than those clowns, which I know is her way of giving me a compliment. The ironic fact is that she's wrong. Those same kids who come into class stoned and with bags of Fritos in their hands instead of their homework are saints compared to Elizabeth Cohen. Even though they stay up late drinking beer and smoking weed, those kids are angels. No matter how bad they are, not a single one of them is guilty of murder.

Our poetry teacher, Ms. Lozano, is famous for sending kids to Kaplan's office. She jokes that there's a revolving door from her classroom to the guidance office. Kids are always writing disturbing sonnets about parental abuse or drugs, or they hand in journal entries that look a little too much like suicide notes, but most of the time these drafts are harmless experiments in adolescent angst. Some kind of preconceived notion that a poem isn't worth reading unless you can tell the poet was sobbing when she wrote it. None of these kids has a regular weekly session with Kaplan the way I do. Ms. Lozano sends them through the revolving door and they come right back with hallway passes and rueful smiles.

I know one girl who wrote disturbing things just to get out of Ms. Lozano's class. She kept handing in poems about how her father beat the crap out of her even though the guy was a pussycat of a man who had never touched a hair on her head. She just liked hanging out in Kaplan's office better than studying Wordsworth and Coleridge. She'd go in there, play with the wooden animals, and chat about the latest baseball scores. Then she'd wander back just before the bell rang. It didn't take long for Kaplan to figure out she was a fake. He told her to get to class and stop scaring the teacher. Now whenever he sees her in the hall, he knocks her on the top of her head with his fist. Not a hard knock, just a little one that means *I'm keeping my eye on you, you twerp.* That's what's good about him. He really gets us.

Kaplan would probably dance a jig if I turned in something depressing like that. He'd probably pay me if Ms. Lozano ever sent me through the revolving door because of my poetry. The more disturbing, the better. *It's therapeutic, Lizzie. You have so many stories that need to be told. Just buy a journal and get them down. Write until it's out of you. Pour your heart into it.*

But lately I've been suffering from chronic writer's block. When Ms. Lozano assigns a poem, I open Tess's Pegasus Journal and hand in something she wrote when we were little kids.

"Which one did you get back today?" Kaplan asks me.

"The one about the selkies. Ms. Lozano said I have a wonderful lyric sensibility. I think it's funny. Tess is getting a B in Ms. Lozano's class even though she's eleven years old. And dead."

Kaplan doesn't smile at my joke. "You need to start handing in your own poetry, Lizzie."

"I don't have my own poetry. I'm bone-dry. I am a stone."

Kaplan smiles and raises one eyebrow. "Listen to the way you speak. Everything you say is a poem."

I put my boots up on his coffee table. "You're just saying that because you don't want me to cheat anymore."

He leans back in his chair and looks across the coffee table at me. "I'm saying it because it's true. Did you hear what you just said to me? Tess was eleven years old when she used the Pegasus Journal. You're fifteen. And in case you haven't noticed, you're alive. If you made an effort to hand in something of your own, I promise you, it would be more powerful than that selkie poem. No offense to your sister's memory, but I happen to think Tess's writing is a bit self-indulgent. You are more mature than she was."

"Not more mature—more boring. Tess had an amazing imagination. That's what made her poems special. I could never be that way."

"She was very ill, Lizzie."

"She was an artist."

"She was delusional. And her poetry was melodramatic. I have the feeling that your own writing would be much more interesting if you gave yourself a chance."

But today isn't a day to give myself a chance. I don't tell Kaplan that today is December 3. The anniversary of Tess's death. I don't tell him about how tonight Mamma will take the yahrzeit candle from the cupboard. We will sit at the table and watch the flames dance. For some reason I want to keep that truth a secret. I want to cup it in my hands and keep it safe like an egg. I want to fold it in the corner of my cheek where it is dark and safe. I stretch out my feet and let my eyes wander out the window where the bare trees scratch the sky like claws.

He opens the Pegasus Journal. Here is the faded paper covered with sketches of selkies dancing in the waves, the moonlight and the water making intricate patterns on their skin. He begins to read her poem. It is strange to hear his familiar voice speak the words my sister wrote so many years ago. Especially on this day, when my memories are so ripe and full they could stand up and walk around, as if I could reach out and touch them. My eyes fill with tears and I listen.

When he's done, Kaplan takes his finger and draws an invisible X across the page. He makes a face like he's smelled something bad. "Do me a favor. Write your own poetry and save the Pegasus Journal for therapy sessions. Time to bury the dead."

"You don't understand," I whisper. "She was brilliant."

"Poor Lizzie," Kaplan says, and his pity stings like a hand slapping my face.

SELKIE

Maiden, walk through waters deep
Sing the waves to kiss your skin
Sunfish fly and fiddlers creep
Turn legs to tail and arms to fin.

The seals remember who you were
So circle 'round, a shining dance
They knew your belly brushed with fur
And dive below to twist and prance.

Phosphorus flash in elfin eyes
Moonlight shivering, sparkling foam
Whirl through wind and seagull's cries
Selkie, float the maiden home.

SELKIE

Here is what most people don't know. In another life, Tess was a selkie who walked out of the ocean and onto the land. She shed her black skin on the shore, her flippers turning into hands and feet, her lovely fingers extending, her long seal-body splitting off to become legs. She left her beautiful black pelt on the shore like a furry bathing suit or pajamas cast off by the rocks, and she danced naked under the full moon until the sun came up. She liked the way it felt to have the salty wind licking her human skin, the soft sand shifting under her bare feet as she danced. But here comes the sad part. Tess says the fishermen stole her beautiful black pelt and now she is trapped in her girl body forever.

"How do you know you were a seal?" We're at the beach near the center of town, standing in the break tides, letting the waves wash over our knees. I love the beach at the very beginning of summer, the quiet expanse of sand, the salty smell, the way my hair whips around my face like seaweed. I wish I were a selkie like Tess. I wish I could climb back into the sea and swim like a seal in the moonlight. I crouch down and let my fingertips fan the cold water like fins. "I think I was a selkie in another life too. I've always been really good at swimming."

Tess laughs. "It's not just about swimming. Selkies are special. You can see it in the face bones." She grabs my chin and examines my profile from both sides. "You don't have the look. You're too human. Selkie bodies look uncomfortable in human skin. See my fingers?" She holds out her skinny hands. I can see the bones in her wrists and elbows. Her arms are covered with fine black hair and her fingers are blue. "These used to be fins. And these too." She raises one string-bean leg and then the other, pointing her toes, raising and lowering each foot so it looks like a flipper. "I'm standing in the water because my body wants to go back. The salt's good for me. It'll keep me alive." Tess cups her hands, dips them into the waves, and swallows seawater. She does this three times. Salt water runs down her chin.

"You're not supposed to drink ocean water," I tell her. "You could get dehydrated. Mamma says the salt will suck all the freshwater out of your body and make you dry up from the inside out. Then you'll really be in trouble."

Tess smiles. "You keep thinking I'm human," she says.

40

I feel my bottom lip quivering. "I want to be a selkie too."

Tess pinches my thigh. "Look at this," she says. Then she pinches my waist and my upper arm. "Look at all this flesh. You're definitely human. No selkie has flesh like this."

I frown. I want to be a selkie more than anything in the world. I want to be special like Tess. "You're wrong," I tell her. "I'm a selkie too. I just kept some of my seal flesh inside and it makes me rounder. I'm just as much a selkie as you are." I feel my eyes fill up with tears, and I take a deep breath to hold them in. I don't want her to see me cry. "I was a selkie in another life too. You don't know everything."

"I know most things."

Tess puts her arm around my shoulders and leans her mouth into the side of my neck so she can whisper. "I know a secret that can help," she says. "There's a special procedure that can turn a human into a seal. It's not easy. It'll hurt. But if you're ready, we could do it. When it's over, we'll both be selkies."

I look back at our parents sitting in their green vinyl beach chairs. Daddy pours iced tea from his thermos into a paper cup. He takes a drink and wipes his beard with the back of his hand. Mamma is editing the pages of her new book with a yellow highlighter, her two lovely feet plunged ankle-deep into the sand, her white linen skirt hiked up above her knees. She moves her arched feet back and forth, comforting herself with the shifting sand, one long pedicured toe scooping out a brown hollow. For a moment I feel sorry for them. They have no idea that their daughters are about to swim away.

"Okay, Tess, I'm ready."

"First we need an alibi. Let me make up a story. I don't want you to say anything."

Tess leads me to the green vinyl chairs where our parents sit side by side, engrossed in words. They are close together, their heads bent over pages, reading out loud. The tips of the pages tremble in the wind. There's something so familiar about their forms that I start to ache before we even get to them.

Daddy leans over to show Mamma a passage that doesn't work. She crosses something out, frowning. Her sun hat slips to the sand. He picks it up by the brim and holds it in his lap. The back of his arm brushes against her knee and she kicks at him with her sandy foot. When they see us approach, they smile at their two wonderful human girls.

"Are you coming for lunch?" Mamma asks us. "We have a thermos filled with iced tea. And there are grapes and potato chips and salami sandwiches. Is anyone hungry? Tess, you didn't have breakfast. I want you to eat something."

"Not right now, Mamma," Tess says. "Lizzie and I want to take a walk. We found a place that's full of humongous blue crabs. I want to see if we can catch them."

Daddy scratches his beard and starts to get up from his chair. "I'll go with you," he grunts. "I need a little exercise. And besides, I think Madam Author has had enough honesty for one morning."

"As long as you come back by lunch," Mamma says.

Daddy pushes his hairy feet into sandals. He taps on the faulty passage once again. She sighs and settles back into her chair with the yellow highlighter. She takes a pencil from behind her ear and begins scribbling something down. Daddy kisses her on the top of her head. "Let's go, girls. You lead the way, Tess."

I look at Tess and bite my lip. Her face is serious, and I can see her mind working.

"Mamma. Please. We want to be alone. Daddy always makes loud noises and they scurry under rocks. It's like crab hunting with a caribou. Please, Mamma. Just me and Lizzie. Daddy's hopeless. Really."

"Humph," says Daddy, pretending to be offended. "I can see when I'm not wanted." He scratches his belly and grins.

"The tide's coming in and you know how the current can get over there by the rocks," Mamma says. "High tide is at twelve-ten. I want you back before that so you can eat a good lunch. Are you hearing me?"

"I have my watch," I tell them, holding up my wrist. "We'll be back for lunch before the tide comes in."

"Sounds fine to me," says Daddy. "Have fun. Be careful."

"Check double-check," says Tess.

I run to Mamma and throw my arms around her. I bury

my face in the space between her shoulder and her neck, a warm scoop that is the perfect size and shape for my head. I imagine this space in her body creating itself and then waiting for my birth to become complete the instant my newborn-baby head nestled in. The wind blows. Her gray hair falls across my cheek. "Bye, Mamma," I whisper. I inhale to keep myself from collapsing. There is the warm scent of lemon and honey.

"Goodness," she says, giving me a squeeze.

Tess grabs my hand and pulls me away before I can change my mind.

She takes me to a place around the bend where the tide is starting to come in over the rocks. We step out of our bathing suits and walk naked and shivering into the water. Tess unties my braids and makes me kneel in the sand. We cup our hands and drink ocean water. Once, twice, three times. She knows I'm worried about drinking the salt. Maybe that won't matter when we are seals. Tess watches me drink, and laughs when the water drips down my chin. Then she tells me to lie on my back and let the waves wash over me.

I am lying naked on my back with my hands raised over my head. The water is filled with icy pinpricks. It stings my skin and makes me want to curl up to protect my private parts, but

Tess tells me the procedure won't work if I wiggle, so I force myself to stay put. Tess is lying motionless in the water next to me. I think she might be getting her seal body already but I don't want to turn my head to check. At first the waves are weak and gentle. They break over our legs and bellies, lapping our shoulders and hips, making our bodies move a little up, a little down, rocking us like babies. The sun is still high in the sky, and with each passing moment my skin becomes colder and colder until I can feel my muscles tense up, my fingers and toes curling. Then I start to lose sensation in my limbs. A burning cold feeling spreads down my arms and legs. The skin on my scalp tenses and I can feel water like an icy hand around my neck.

The waves grow. They crash white and sizzling like silver needles all around us. One wave washes over my face. I sputter and cough. The salt burns my throat, but I force myself to lie still like Tess told me. I fight an urge to struggle to my knees. When the next wave comes, I'm ready for it. I hold my breath. Our bodies drift toward the rocks where the current is strongest. Tess is still except for the motion of the water. She isn't even moving her hands to keep herself afloat. When a wave washes over her, she keeps her eyes open.

I wish I were like Tess. She knows how to be certain about things. She doesn't keep herself up at night wondering if she said or did the right thing. She just believes. For Tess the world makes sense. Everything that happens contains a secret meaning. A white butterfly means good luck. A sand dollar means watch your step. A warm wind means Merlin is whispering. Nothing means anything to me. When I see a seagull, it doesn't tell me anything. The sun hurts my eyes. And even these waves are just waves after half an hour of floating, naked and cold.

No part of me is turning into a seal. I am just as human as I was when we started. I still have arms and legs and skin and flesh and hair, and everything hurts from the cold. Now I am shivering so hard that my teeth rattle and my breath comes in jagged gasps. My eyes sting with tears of disappointment. Tess was right. I am human. I am not magical like she is. I'm ordinary ordinary ordinary.

I struggle to my knees and look for my bathing suit. It's draped over the top of a toothy rock. When we started the transformation, the entire rock jutted out of the water. Now all I can see is the very tip, an arrow pointing to the sky. A wave breaks over me and knocks me back down. Then another one. Larger. It washes into my mouth. I can feel my forehead slam against stone, barnacles dragging my cheek. I make it to my feet. Another wave crashes into me and another.

"Tess!" I screech. "Tess!"

I can't see her.

I whirl around, looking for her body. She had been so still.

Then the thought comes to me. She has turned into a seal. She has turned into a seal and swum away. I'll never see her again.

What will I tell Mamma and Daddy?

How will I explain what she has done?

I push my way through the water toward the rock where our bathing suits are draped. I struggle to put mine on. My legs and arms are so weak I can barely do it, and tears are streaming from my eyes and my breath is coming in shaky, chattering gasps. My cheek is bleeding. I touch my face and my fingers come away red. Red blossoms in the water and stains the sand when I finally struggle to the shore. I am coughing. I kneel down in the sand and heave salt water from my stomach. The ocean pours out of my mouth.

Then I look up.

Tess is standing there with her hands on her hips.

"I guess the magic didn't work," she says.

Tess helps me to my feet.

She reaches out and wipes blood off my cheek. Then she takes her cloth ponytail holder from around her wrist and holds it against my face. She presses it into my cheek until the bleeding slows and then stops. "I know it hurts," she says, her voice low and soothing. "You're going to be okay."

I watch her step back into her bathing suit. Her body is all angles—ankles, knees, elbows, collarbone. She takes me by the hand. I am still shaking and unable to speak. We walk silently down the beach, our footsteps filling with sand behind us, all the way back to green vinyl chairs where Mamma and Daddy are still sitting side by side, their heads bent over the tattered pages. The corners bend and curl in the wind.

KITCHEN GHOSTS

Daddy spends more time at the Boat House every year. At first he came home at five, right on time for dinner. Then it was seven or eight. Lately, he doesn't come home until long after me and Mamma have whispered our good-nights and gone up to bed. Most nights now, I wake to hear the sound of his truck, then the crunch of his boots up the hill and across the fallen leaves outside our porch. He falls asleep on the couch with the newspaper folded over his belly and a bottle of beer on the side table. He claims he stays late sanding or staining, or soaking the ribs of the antique boats so they bend the right way, but I know this is a lie. The real reason he stays late is that he doesn't want to sit at the dinner table with me and Mamma. He doesn't want to listen to the clink of silverware, or the whine of the radiator, or the tick of the clock above the stove counting away the seconds: sounds we never noticed when the house was full of Tess.

Do me a favor. Write your own poetry and save the Pegasus Journal for therapy sessions. Time to bury the dead.

The first years after it happened, Daddy tried to make conversation. "How was your day at school, Lizzie?" he would ask. "I saw Mrs. Caruso at the coffee shop. She asked after you. Said you haven't visited her in a while." Or he would try to make Mamma smile. "Nando says *Sea Shanty*'s still selling strong. Not just to tourists. Locals are asking for it too. Lobstermen and dockworkers. They love how you describe the ocean. Isn't that wonderful? Lillian Cohen. The fishermen's author." And she would nod and offer some halfhearted story about her day. She edited all the adjectives out of chapter six. She watched a cormorant sun itself on the pier. She bought a new laundry detergent. But as the months and years passed and the silence yawned wider, Mamma's daily recollections became shorter until, finally, they faded away to the clink of silverware, the sound of swallowing.

Do me a favor. Write your own poetry and save the Pegasus Journal for therapy sessions. Time to bury the dead.

Today, after school I walk behind the docks to the Boat House. I hunch my shoulders while I walk. Kaplan's words echo in my ears. I carry Tess's Pegasus Journal in the inside pocket of my coat the same way I did five years ago. I can feel the hard corner jabbing into my ribs like a bony finger or the blunt edge of a knife or the toe of my sister's foot. *Time to bury the dead. Time to bury the dead.* I remember Tess's burial. The rabbi helped me shovel the dirt into her grave. There was the terrifying thump of dirt falling on the coffin. Then Uncle Morris and Mamma's cousin Max and Daddy took turns with the shovel. We stood in a circle and watched the dirt fill in the hole. I imagined Tess's white face with her eyes sewn shut.

I open the door of the Boat House, and for a moment I can forget the fact that today is the anniversary of Tess's death. Here I am surrounded by familiar things. In the corner by the door is the old wooden fisherman still holding his rod with the same grinning fish dangling from the line. Here is the antique compass, the same one they've had since I was a little girl. And here behind the same scratched desk sits Daddy's assistant, Mr. Gagliardi, who is still fat and bald, and who still smokes too many cigarettes, and who still flirts with me the same way he has done since I was old enough to laugh and smile and pull away.

"Well well well," he rasps, taking a puff of his cigarette. "Look at what the cat dragged in. You're gettin' real pretty, Lizzie. Just like your mamma."

"Is my dad here?" I ask him.

"Out back. Go on ahead. Yes sirree, real pretty. You're what, twenty-five, twenty-six now?"

It's the same joke he's been telling since I was a toddler.

"Fifteen," I tell him, smiling.

Mr. Gagliardi scratches his bald head and then repositions his suspenders over his huge belly. "Fifteen? Is that all? Well, I guess I'll just have to wait a few more years to ask you out. Whaddaya say, Lizzie? I'm your type, ain't I? Handsome and rich?" He laughs a deep, throaty laugh and puckers up like he wants me to give him a kiss.

"You said Daddy's out back?"

"Yup. Careful of the sawhorse. And make sure to close the door all the way. It's cold out there. Boy oh boy. You look more like your mamma every time you set foot in here. She broke my heart too, you know. Long time ago."

"I know," I say. "You've told me before. See you later, Mr. Gagliardi." I inch past him the way I always do, past the invoices and sketches of boats with arrows and measurements, past the smell of tobacco and sawdust, past the rubber boots, past the raincoats hanging on their hooks, and out the door to the boatyard where the huge hulls of Daddy's antique boats lie open like whale bones, washed up on the docks. I always loved this place. When we were little, Tess and I used to make up fairy stories behind the boats while Daddy worked. Sometimes we climbed inside and pretended we were being kidnapped by pirates. We would lie down on our backs and listen to Daddy's hammer and the songs of seagulls winging overhead. *They're the ghosts of all the people who drowned at sea,* Tess told me. *If you listen, you can hear them tell how they died. Rainstorm. Rainstorm. Rainstorm. Pirates. Pirates. Pirates. Lightning. Lightning. Lightning.*

Time to bury the dead.

Daddy looks up from his work and smiles when he sees me coming. He has sawdust in his hair and in his beard. He wears an old cable-knit sweater and muddy work boots.

"Come over here," he says.

I pick up a rag from the dock and make my way to where he's working. He wipes his hands and then gives me a bear hug. He smells like salt and sawdust. I relax into him, resting my head against his beard like I used to do when I was little, but then I pull away to look at him. He's getting old. There are wrinkles at the corners of his eyes. Daddy holds my hands and looks at me too. "Your hair is too long," he says. "Pull it away from your face. You should let people see how pretty you are." He pulls my hair back into a ponytail with one hand. "There," he says, "now you look like your mamma."

"I like it down," I say.

"It makes you look unkempt. I have ten dollars in my pocket. Go down to Pondolfino's. Get yourself a haircut."

"You're the one who needs to clean up, Daddy," I tell him. "Why don't you use the ten bucks on yourself? Get a haircut and a shave. Come home to Mamma tonight. She misses you. We both miss you. We should be together tonight, Daddy."

Daddy picks up a piece of sandpaper from the dock and begins working it across the plank. His red calloused hands push and pull. He puts his weight into it, and the fine golden sawdust falls to the dock. "I'm almost done with this frame," he tells me, gesturing to the empty hull. "She was a whaling ship. More than a hundred and fifty years old. Can you imagine that? Look at the carved wood. She's beautiful."

"Daddy," I say. "Mamma's going to light the yahrzeit candle tonight."

He stops and looks at me. His eyes are red. "I know," he says.

Then he reaches out and touches my face. We stand there for a moment, looking at each other. Not saying anything. Then he turns away.

"There's a lot of work to be done here," he says. "Tomorrow and Friday there's going to be rain. That'll set me back some. I want to finish the hull so I can start putting the boards back up on her sides. Then she'll really come together."

I watch him sanding. He moves his hands back and forth

along the plank. The sawdust falls like snow across the wooden boards. Then he stops. "We need the money, Lizzie," he tells me. "If I get her done ahead of schedule there's a bonus. It'll come in handy once winter hits. I'm almost finished. One week. Two weeks, tops."

I nod. My hair falls down over my eyes. Daddy reaches over, pulls it back into a ponytail again. "You look just like her, you know." I'm not sure if he is talking about Tess or Mamma. I bend my head to the side and rest my cheek against his hand. It's rough and cold, chapped from the wind. I want to cry so badly I can taste the salt in my mouth. I can feel the heat coming into my cheeks and eyes. But I hold my body still and make myself go distant.

Time to bury the dead. Time to bury the dead.

"You still meeting with that doctor every Wednesday?" he asks me.

"Yes," I whisper.

"Is it helping any?"

Inside my jacket, the Pegasus Journal pushes into my ribs like a fist.

"Yes," I tell him. "It's helping."

Daddy kisses my forehead. "Good," he says. "You keep talking to that doctor. You tell him everything you need to say."

A seagull lands on the pier and looks at us. "Tell Mamma I'll be home late tonight," Daddy says. He pushes a ten-dollar bill into my hand. "For the haircut," he tells me. Then he bends his head over the plank, works the sandpaper back and forth along the wood.

———

When I come home, Mamma is standing at the window.

"I saw Daddy at the Boat House today," I tell her softly. "He said he'll be home late."

"Your father works hard." Mamma squares her shoulders. She pushes a strand of gray hair behind her ear and moves away from the window.

It's cold in the house tonight. Even with the woodstove going, there's a chill and I'm shivering under my sweater. Mamma opens the cupboard. She takes out the yahrzeit candle in a little glass jar. She lights it with a match and brings it to the kitchen table. We sit in silence and watch the shadows dance.

When the silence becomes unbearable, Mamma brings bowls of vegetable soup and a plate piled high with grilled cheese sandwiches. The steam rises toward the wooden beams in the ceiling. Mamma looks at me and tries to smile. "I made a special soup tonight," she says. "The vegetables were frozen from Mrs. Caruso's garden. A little taste of summer on a winter night. Have some before it gets cold. It's good."

I drink soup. Mamma drinks soup. Our spoons clink against the yawning bowls.

"These vegetables are great," I tell Mamma. "Mrs. Caruso should win an award for these vegetables."

Mamma nods. She raises a spoon to her lips. I can hear the sound of her tongue and throat working to swallow. Then she smiles weakly as an idea occurs to her. "I can't grow anything," she says. "Do you remember the peach trees I planted out back? Those peaches were so furry they tasted like cat's paws."

"I don't think this is the right climate for peach trees."

"No," she says, "I guess not. But I did have nice cucumbers one summer. It was a miracle. Seven rows of cucumber vines. We were eating cucumber pickles from that garden for months. Your daddy loved them." Mamma laughs a soft, broken laugh. "Maybe I'm not so bad at growing things after all."

"No," I say, smiling. "You're good at growing cucumbers. And novels. Just not peach trees."

"Right. Cucumbers and novels. And daughters." Mamma smiles with watery eyes. "I grew you, Lizzie. And you turned out okay. Not as good as the cucumbers maybe, but nowhere near as bad as the peaches."

It's a joke. She reaches across the table to touch my hand. Her fingers are cold and smooth. I try to smile, but tears are coming to my eyes and I have to hold my breath to keep them back. Mamma gets up from her seat. She walks around the table to where I'm sitting on the wooden stool with my half-empty bowl of vegetable soup and my half-finished triangle of grilled cheese. She stands behind me. I can feel the sudden warmth of her body close to my back and shoulders. She wraps her

arms around me. She buries her face in my hair. She breathes
and breathes.

"Mamma," I say.

She doesn't answer. Now she is combing her hands through
my hair and rocking me back and forth. The candle glows in
its glass jar. I feel like I'm going to split open.

"Mamma," I say. "Mamma, stop."

She stops. She takes her hands off me and backs away.

"I need to get my homework done," I mutter.

I bring my bowl and my plate to the sink.

Mamma goes to the window. She looks out toward the
empty driveway. Her shoulders are thin. She holds herself.

"It really was good soup," I say. "Those vegetables were delicious."

Mamma keeps watching out the window. She stares down
the hill to the river. Behind her the kitchen table waits with
its four empty chairs hidden in the shadows of candlelight.

QUEEN OF TOADS

Ghosts of toads still haunt my dreams
Scratch my cheeks with desperate nails
Leather lips still jeer and scream
And mouths drip blood on muddy trails.

QUEEN OF TOADS

In July after it rains, our garden is filled with hoptoads. We can see them if we squat down by the cucumber vines where the leaves twist and twirl. They crouch in the wet mud and blow bubbles, their cheeks puffing like tiny white balloons. We kneel in the dirt, really still and quiet, so they won't suspect that anything is going to happen. Tess is the queen of toads. She tells me how to do it. I cup my right hand with all my fingers together. Then I drop right down on them like a red-tailed hawk. *Whap*. So they don't see it coming. I can feel them hopping around down there, trying to get out of the cave of my fingers, but I don't let them out. I slide my left hand underneath, ever so slowly, inch by inch, so the wet garden under their feet turns to skin, and before they know it they are sitting right in my palm with my top hand still cupped like a cave. Sometimes they find it so exciting that they pee. And that's the part I like the most.

Tess has the red Radio Flyer wagon and she is scooping up toads and filling the wagon with squirming bodies. Before long, there are so many toads I can barely see the rusty bottom. All I can see are the tiny brown creatures, small as stones, trying to get themselves up and over the edge. They stretch up on their skinny toes and push their white tummies onto the wall of the wagon, but they can't get out. They are too small. When Tess isn't looking I smell my palm, damp from happy hoptoads. My skin smells golden and dizzy like summer.

"Are you ready?" Tess asks me. She is breathless and her eyes are shining.

"Of course I'm ready." I wipe my hands on my ripped shorts and we set off. Tess goes first. She holds the wooden handle and drags the wagon down the pine needle path and onto Little River Road. I trail behind, making sure none of the hoptoads escape. The sun beats down on our bare shoulders. It takes half an hour to make our way down the cracked concrete road and up the hill into the woods to each fisherman's cottage, dragging the red wagon between us with the hoptoads squirming from the heat. Tess knocks on each door and stands in front so that the women see her white smile first when the screen door opens.

When we get to Mrs. Caruso's cottage, she comes out on her front steps in her floral housedress and puts her ham-hock hands on her hips. She looks like a swollen apple someone left on the windowsill for too long, all tired and brown. I scoop up a toad from the wagon and cup it in my hands.

"Oh my goodness," she says. "What have my two favorite girls brought for me today? Come on up. Careful on the stairs. There you go."

Mrs. Caruso has more cats than you can count. A whole yowling chorus. A feline symphony. It didn't start that way. At first, Mrs. Caruso just put out one bowl of milk a day for the strays. They lapped up the milk she set out in saucers on the porch steps. But then the strays had kittens and those kittens had kittens and before anyone could blink, that old porch was covered with cats. There are cats curled up like doughnuts all over the porch. On the wicker chair, the porch swing, the railing, the welcome mat. When they hear our footsteps, they begin to uncurl and stretch their bodies.

"We're selling toads," I tell her, but my salesman voice comes out shy, so I show her what's hiding in my hands. A black-and-white kitten rubs himself against my legs. "Five cents each. Six for a quarter." The toad hops onto her porch. He sits there and blows bubbles. The cat looks hungry.

Mrs. Caruso smiles and I can see her gums. "This has got to be Tess Cohen's idea, am I right? My girls used to sell lemonade on hot days. Used to set up right down there by the docks. What about a lemonade stand? Does your mamma still have those scrawny little lemon trees out back? Oh no. That's right. They're peach trees. The fruits just look like lemons." She slaps her thighs and laughs. It's a good joke.

Tess steps forward. She has captured the toad and now she

is holding it inches away from the old woman's face. She is breathing hard and her eyes are flashing. "Toads are good for gardens," she tells Mrs. Caruso. "They eat Japanese beetles. They fertilize the ground. Plus they make cute pets. This little guy likes to be scratched between the eyes. We'll sell him to you for three cents. That's a bargain. Buy some toads, Mrs. Caruso. You won't regret it."

Mrs. Caruso pushes Tess's skinny hand away from her face. She is laughing her crooked laugh. "Now I've heard it all," she says. "Okay, *bella*. I'll take two. You say they're good for gardens? Why not. Maybe I'll have better tomatoes this year. Or maybe these kitties will have a snack." She puts her hand into her apron pocket and fishes out two nickels. I count the change while Tess puts her toads in a plastic baggie. They look dry and drowsy. They move their back legs and make their eyes go half closed. Mrs. Caruso opens the bag to let them breathe.

"You better set them free so they can start doing their magic," says Tess, all up in her face again.

The old woman gives Tess a kiss.

"Thank you very much, Mrs. Caruso," I say. "See you soon."

"Enjoy the toads," sings Tess. "And good luck with those tomatoes. I bet they'll be the juiciest, sweetest tomatoes you've had in fifty years."

"Well, I sure hope so. If they're good, I'll have you to thank." Mrs. Caruso waves as we climb back down the splintering wooden steps. A skinny calico hisses at us and darts under the porch. We take the wagon and then make our way down the pine needle path and back to Little River Road, where the heat makes the cracked road ripple and bend. "Give my regards to your parents," the old woman calls down the hill. "Tell your mamma to stop being such a stranger."

We wave and smile. The red Radio Flyer wagon clatters along on the cracked road and the sun shines down on our bare shoulders. I can hear the high, lazy whine of seagulls swooping around the fishing boats and the clang of buoys on the river.

We have coins jingling around in our pockets, and they are hot like a fat old lady's been breathing on them. Sal's Corner Store is just up the street. If you add Tess's twenty-seven cents and my six cents, we have enough to split a grape double Popsicle. There's nothing like a double Popsicle on a hot day. It makes the inside of your mouth chilly, and when you inhale fast, it feels like you're bringing refrigerator air into your lungs.

Tess breaks our double Popsicle in half so that we each have one stick. We sit on the blue-and-red vinyl swirly stools and lick the Popsicles. There's a fan on the tin ceiling of the store and it cools the sweat off our backs. Tess knows how to swirl so that her braids stick straight out and you can barely see her through the blur of her turning. I stop her by sticking out my foot and she kicks my foot away. She tilts her head to the ceiling and laughs. I love the sound of her laughter. We sit in Sal's Corner Store and watch the customers come and go. We watch Sal at the cash register, punching in numbers and pressing the bell so the drawer shoots out. We lick our Popsicles and we twirl and twirl until we've forgotten all about the heat. We've forgotten all about the toads. We've forgotten all about Mrs. Caruso. All we can think about is how our lips are sweet with purple grape double Popsicles, and how our skin is smooth from all that air blowing around, and we are dizzy and giggling from twirling.

When St. Mary's bell strikes three, we open the door and step outside onto the scalding road. The sun is so bright we squint our eyes. It bakes the concrete, licking its heat across everything: the fishermen's cottages, the old wooden docks, the stone pilings, the pyramids of lobster traps. Everything bends and ripples from the heat like it's underwater, and for a moment, it seems as though Little River is holding its breath from all that heat, like it doesn't want to draw the air into its scorched lungs. I stand behind the red Radio Flyer wagon and wait for Tess to take up the wooden handle. That is when I hear her voice.

"Oh no, Lizzie," Tess rasps. "Oh no, Lizzie. The toads."

The red Radio Flyer wagon is still parked right in the sun where we left it. The wooden handle is still propped up against the crumbling redbrick side of Sal's Corner Store. I drop down next to Tess to look at the reason her voice sounds so sad. And then I see the awful thing we've done. Every toad is dead. Every single toad has been baked alive against the scalding metal. They are flattened out on the bottom of the wagon, their dried-up bodies brown and leathery, stuck fast to the rusted bottom. Some of them are plastered against the wall where they must have tried to get out. Some have open mouths. Some have open eyes. Some have one leg lifted, one claw clenched. I have never seen so many dead bodies. I touch them with one finger, really gently so that they don't fall apart. They are warm and dry and studded with perfect brown warts, their fingernails brittle as pine needles.

Tess is sobbing. Her breath comes in short gasps and tears stream down her cheeks. She looks at me wordlessly.

I put my arm around her shoulders and pick up the wooden handle of the red Radio Flyer wagon. We walk slowly, step by step, heads bowed, back down Little River Road, the wagon like a hearse clattering behind us. We pass by the old docks on one side and the fishermen's cottages on the other, and, in between, the cracked concrete road stretches on toward the harbor. The late-afternoon sun beats down, hot, golden, and unforgiving as a funeral.

When evening comes, it is low tide, and there's no breeze coming up from the river. The floating docks and rowboats sit at the muddy bottom waiting for the tide to lift them back past the reeds and the clam beds. The sun's going down, and there's a kind of milky after-light, almost orange, all down the river.

Mamma and Daddy are sitting on the wooden porch-swing

not saying anything, just swinging slowly. Daddy has his binoculars. He's watching a flock of egrets take off from the mud bank, their wings breaking the silence like applause. Mamma's got her feet curled up under her skirt, and she's leaning on Daddy's shoulder. Her eyes are closed, but I know she's not sleeping. She's listening to the evening sounds and feeling the slightest breath of wind on her neck, and she's thinking how lucky she is to have two beautiful girls like me and Tess. She has no idea that we still have the cruel murder of an entire wagon full of hoptoads on our hands. Even after we scraped the bodies off the rusty bottom, even after we filled it with salt water and scrubbed it down with laundry soap, it still smelled like corpses.

Tess is sitting on the bottom porch stair. She has the Pegasus Journal open across her bare knees and she's scribbling pictures of vengeful toads and writing poem lines. The toads have leathery faces and wild, rolling eyes and they reach out with fingers thin and sharp as wire. I come and sit down next to her with my glass of ice water. I drink from my straw and watch her sketch. Her pencil flies across the page. I wish I could draw like Tess. Whenever I draw, I make the outline first. When a line goes in the wrong place, I erase it. I blow on the rubber filings and wipe the page off with the side of my hand and then I blow and wipe again before I try to get the line in right. Tess doesn't even bother with outlines. She goes straight for the shadows, for the spaces between one thing and another. She scribbles and scratches and rubs in colors. I lean my head on her shoulder and watch the toads appear from the shadows with their mouths open and snarling.

"That's really scary, Tess," I whisper.

Tess makes a toad with two little girls huddled together inside its jeering mouth. They clutch each other. Their faces are terrified. She rubs her thumb across the page and suddenly the shadows close in like secrets across the white, untouched paper. Soon, even the shadows are gone. All I can see are the blurred outlines of girls and toads, their bodies smearing into each other. Her hands are moving so quickly that her breath comes out of her mouth in short rasping breaths. I run my hand through her hair the way Mamma does when she wants to make us hush. I touch her cheek with the back of my thumb. Her skin is ice-cold.

Mamma looks at us sitting together and sighs. She buries her face in Daddy's beard and he puts his arm around her shoulders. The binoculars dangle from their black leather cord. My parents don't speak to each other. Time passes this way. Mamma and Daddy rocking and looking out at the water. Me with my arm around Tess. Down in the river, the tide is coming in. The bands of water become wider and deeper until finally, imperceptibly, the boats and docks begin to rise back into the river. Overhead, a seagull screams. I pull Tess close while she sketches. I hold her and I don't let go.

RUMPELSTILTSKIN

Lullaby, thou feline beast
Cross thy paws, thy eyelids creased
Tail tucked tender 'neath thy nose
Mrow and mumble, purr and pose.

If I could, I'd lick thy fur
Taste thy breath and slurp thy purr
I would clean between thy toes
Mrow and mumble, purr and pose.

Come and curl up in my arms
Cast thy sleep spell, snore thy charms
Whiskers whisk while moonlight glows
Mrow and mumble, purr and pose.

RUMPELSTILTSKIN

Sometimes when we go over to Mrs. Caruso's house we bring her a gift. One time we brought a dandelion crown that Tess placed on her balding head like a golden halo. Another time we brought her a woolly bear caterpillar that walked across her wrinkled palm and made her laugh so hard she lost her dentures. But today is special, because today we bring her the best present of all. Tess has picked five green peaches from Mamma's trees out back, and I crushed them with a rock, and we put all that mushy pulp into a glass with water and sugar and ice. Then we tied a pink ribbon around the glass and brought it over to her porch. "Here's your lemonade, Mrs. Caruso," Tess says, smiling at her, sweet as can be. "Just like your daughters used to make." And instead of saying thanks but no thanks, like any other old lady would do, she drinks it all down in one gulp, wipes her lips, and says "Mmmm. Peachy. Got any more?"

We always stay and play with the cats until Mamma calls us to come on home. But Mrs. Caruso doesn't mind. She's lonely ever since Mr. Caruso didn't make it back from a lobster run. The waves ripped him from the *Sweet Charity* and swallowed him whole, cracking the white skiff wide open across the rocks. They never found his body, but they did find three of the traps washed up on the shore with a whole load of lobsters still in them.

Some of Mrs. Caruso's cats are friendly. These are the ones that were people's pets a long time ago, the fat ones, who still remember how good it feels to be scratched behind the ears. The friendly cats run down the stairs to meet us when we walk by and push their bodies into our legs. They let us pick them up without hissing and, sometimes, if we sit quietly on the grass, they curl up in our laps and purr.

Tess loves the feral cats best, the wild cats that don't trust anybody. These are the cats who were born under the porch or in the piles of rope out back. They sleep under the broken row-boats or in the bottoms of barrels. They have never been inside. They mince across the porch with their little round bellies and spindly legs, and hiss at us when we hold out our hands. If we call to them, they dart under wicker chairs. Feral cats are never just one color. They are butterscotch and white. They are stripy and splotched. Patchwork cats. Tess has a name for each one. Finn has a broken tail and ragged ears. Yellow Belly is always pregnant. Rumpelstiltskin is so skinny his pelvis pokes out and the tip of his tail is pencil thin.

Tess has a plastic baggie of leftover pickled herring for the cats. After Mrs. Caruso finishes her lemonade, we tiptoe down to her scraggly front lawn and wait for a wild cat to get brave. I try to get Yellow Belly to come over, but every time I hold out my hand she yowls at me and hisses. Tess has her eye on Rumpelstiltskin. She pitches tidbits of herring into the pine needles and he creeps closer with each bite. You can tell he's starving by the way he gobbles up the fish, with his eyes closed. Tess sits Indian-style in the pine needles. Every once in a while she makes a low purring sound that comes from the back of her throat, and Rumpelstiltskin twitches his ears and takes a few uneasy steps forward.

Mrs. Caruso stands on the porch in her floral housedress. She puts her hands on her hips. "Holy Mother," she says. "If I didn't see it with my own eyes, I wouldn't believe it. Tess Cohen, I've known that cat since he was born and he has never come within three feet of me. You must have the magic touch." She lowers her body down onto the porch swing and whistles through her missing teeth. "Look at him, Lizzie. He's eating right off her foot."

Tess grins but doesn't move. She has lined her bare foot with pickled herring tidbits and Rumpelstiltskin is eating them one at a time with dainty paws. He's purring, and his pencil-thin tail flicks one way and the other. Tess purrs too. He lets her scratch him under his chin.

"I can't get any of the wild cats to come over to me," I

complain. "They always like Tess better. All animals like Tess."

"Your sister speaks their language. Listen to her purr. I would have thought she was a cat herself if I didn't know better."

"I can purr just as good as Tess," I say.

"Of course you can," Mrs. Caruso says, her voice going all sugary and apologetic. "Don't be sad, *bella*. I didn't mean anything by it. I just enjoy that sister of yours. She's different. I have an idea, Lizzie. Why don't you come up on the porch and rock with me awhile? I think that skinny stray is gonna let your sister pick him up and it'll be fun to watch from up here. Front-row seats. You come up now, *bellezza*. Nice and quiet."

I shuffle up the stairs and settle in beside her. She smells like talcum powder and roses, and when she pulls me in beside her, she's warm and fat like a feather pillow. Pretty soon I'm leaning my head on her shoulder and feeling sleepy. The swing goes back and forth. We watch Tess work her magic with the little cat. He eats off her toe, off her foot, off her knee— and before we know it, he's standing in her lap and taking herring right from her hand. Tess makes a high, sad, mewing sound and Rumpelstiltskin mews back. He stretches and then curls up in her lap. Soon he is giving himself a bath with a scratchy pink tongue, purring and purring. He licks his paws, his tail, and then finally the inside of my sister's skinny arm.

Tess meows. She opens her mouth, sticks out her own red tongue, and begins to lick him back. She cleans him like a mamma cat. The top of his dusty head, the torn-up ears, the bald patch between his skinny shoulder blades. She closes her eyes and licks all the way down his back.

"Tess Cohen, I think you'd better stop that," Mrs. Caruso says in a loud whisper. "That kitty hasn't ever had shots, and he's probably got fleas. You can pet him, but I don't think licking him is a good idea."

Tess ignores her. She's got her head down in her lap and she is licking and purring and sort of rocking back and forth. Rumpelstiltskin rolls over and Tess begins to lick his belly.

"Lizzie, what in God's name is that girl doing?"

"She really likes animals," I whisper.

"That sister of yours is going to get worms. Or worse. Tess Cohen, if you don't stop that disgusting circus show, I will call your mamma and she'll have your hide."

My heart skips a beat.

Tess licks lower.

"Stop it!" I screech.

Rumpelstiltskin yowls and slashes Tess across the face. Then he darts under the house and hunches up, growling. Tess is bleeding from the gash in her cheek, but she still has the same dreamy grin on her face and her tongue is still sticking out from between her lips. I run down the porch steps and pull her to her feet. Mrs. Caruso is standing on the porch with her hands on her hips, looking down at us. "Tess Cohen, you put your tongue back in your mouth and stop that smiling. You look like a retard."

Tess looks right through the old woman as though she were a window. Her eyes are glazed. She's making that purring sound deep down in the back of her throat, and when I pull her close to me she rubs her head against mine and licks the scar on my cheek with her wet tongue. It's the place where the barnacles scraped against my skin, and it tingles and warms. Tess is bleeding. I can see the long, red cat scratch. The blood makes a crimson line from her cheek to her jaw.

"Lick me," Tess intones in a voice that sounds more like a meow.

I look up at Mrs. Caruso and smile weakly. "She gets really into things," I tell her. "Like right now she's pretending to be a cat. She's good at pretending, aren't you, Tess. I'm good at pretending too."

"Lick me."

"Lizzie," the old woman says, her voice full of something I don't understand.

"Lick me, Lizzie," says Tess. "Do it. Now."

There are tears in my eyes. I hear the creak of Mrs. Caruso making her way down the front steps, but before she can get to us I take Tess's face in both hands. I lean over and lick her long, red cat scratch with the tip of my tongue. It tastes like the ocean.

COUNTING CROWS

One for sorrow, two for bliss
Three for serpent's mournful hiss
Four for treasure, five for tricks
Six for the rose that pulls and pricks
Seven in the garden, eight in the sea
Nine for the nine that watch from the tree
Nightmares are silver, dreams are gold
Ten for the wish in ignorance told.

COUNTING CROWS

Some girls have birthdays they celebrate in style year after year. They get white tablecloths, colorful balloons, and a flock of pretty guests who arrive in party dresses with long hair tied back. First they play games like pin the tail on the donkey and statues. Then there is the piñata and the candy and the presents and the ice cream in little paper cups. When it's over, they leave with smiling faces. *Thank you, thank you, come again next year.* But my birthday has never been like that. There have never been other kids living on the river. Just retired fishermen and widows and summer people who come and go like mushrooms. The only person I ever invite to my birthday is Mrs. Caruso on account of the fact that she is my only friend who is not also my sister.

Today is August 1. I am ten years old today, which means that today I am the birthday queen. Mamma brings a bowl of green peaches onto the porch, all cut up in triangles just the way I like. She gives me a kiss on the top of my head. Daddy is sitting on the railing with his beat-up guitar, playing bluegrass notes that dance and twirl on the breeze. It's a good day to turn a year older. Up in the pine trees, there are three crows telling jokes and pounding each other on the back with crooked wings.

"I smell a ten-year-old girl!" someone shouts to us from down the hill. We run to the railing to see Mrs. Caruso coming up with a picnic basket overflowing with tomatoes. "I thought I would bring them on your birthday." She huffs up the hill, one hand on the hem of her skirt, the other grasping the handle of the basket.

"Best tomatoes I've grown in years," she says, out of breath. "You girls were right. Those toads were magic. Kitty cats ate them for supper one day and pooped them out in the garden the next." She stops halfway up to cough and spit in the pine needles. I run down to give her my arm and help her up the rest of the way. She leans into me and squeezes my hand. "They're the reddest, juiciest tomatoes I've ever seen. I tell you, Lizzie, you girls and me, we could go into business. Cohen and Caruso. Sure enough."

I walk her up the stairs to the porch where Mamma and Daddy and Tess are waiting. She lowers her body into an Adirondack chair.

Tess selects the reddest tomato in the basket and places it into my hands with a regal flourish. "Your highness," she says.

I hold it up to my nose. It smells like August, like dirt and sun, like the warm brown backs of summer toads. I bite in. It is delicious. Salty. The juice drips down my chin. I wipe it off with the back of my hand. "It's perfect," I say.

Tess pulls me to the hammock. We lie side by side, sharing bites of the birthday tomato and pushing our feet into the railing so the hammock swings us back and forth. The wind stirs our hair with gentle fingers.

"I don't know if you people have heard the news," says Mrs. Caruso. "A family just bought the old Pondolfino place. See down there? They've already taken the sign down. I saw them walking around in there the other day. There are a lot of them. A whole boatload of boys. And there's a girl Lizzie's age, going into fifth grade in a few weeks. You wild little girls are going to have some neighbor kids to civilize you. What do you think of that?"

My heart skips a beat.

There is a moment of silence. A pause when nobody says anything.

Tess kicks her foot into the porch rail and shouts, "We don't need neighbor kids!"

"Watch your tone," warns Daddy.

Tess leaps out of the hammock. She skulks away and flops down on the front stairs, hugging her knees. I swing back and forth without her.

"They're in their own world most of the time," Mamma explains, smiling apologetically. "They've never really needed other kids. But I think it would be good for the girls to branch out a bit. No harm in that, right, Tess?"

Tess puts her hands over her ears.

Mamma sighs. Then she offers Mrs. Caruso the plate of sliced, almost-ripe peaches. "Here, Stella. Have a green peach. Lizzie loves them. Don't ask me why."

Mrs. Caruso bites in. "You sure know how to grow a good green peach, Lillian. You got to tell me how you do it one of these days."

Mamma laughs and puts her hand on Mrs. Caruso's arm. "We really should see more of each other, Stella," she says. "Maybe I'd finally learn something about gardening."

"I keep telling you, Lillian. I'm just down the road. You don't have to be a stranger."

"Oh I know," says Mamma. "I always think about visiting. But time gets away from me."

Daddy knocks on the wood of his guitar and then goes on playing.

Soon Mamma disappears into the kitchen and then comes back out with a sad little green peach pie all sunken in the middle. There are ten lit candles on top. Daddy stops playing, and we watch the flames dance in the wind.

Tess breaks the silence. "Blow them out. Blow them out," she says.

"Make a wish," says Daddy.

I close my eyes and wish the biggest wish I've ever wished.

Then I blow with cheeks like a puffer fish.

All the candles go out. *Huff.* Just like that.

Mamma kisses me on the top of the head. "Happy birthday."

"What did you wish?" Daddy asks me.

"Don't tell," whispers Tess at my elbow. "It won't come true."

But Mamma and Daddy and Mrs. Caruso are smiling at me, and the sun is shining, and crows are laughing in the pine trees, and somewhere down by the river I can hear a fishing boat coming in. Everything feels like heaven. Mamma gives us paper plates and serves up the pie. It is sour and green, just how I like it.

"You know what I wished?" I ask them.

"We don't need to know," says Tess.

"I wished that every day of my year will be just as good as this day."

"That's my girl," Mamma says.

The notes of Daddy's guitar rise into the air like smoke.

"Now you've ruined it," Tess mumbles into her knees.

"Tess," says Mamma disapprovingly.

Mrs. Caruso takes Mamma's arm. "Let's take a peek at your garden," she says gently.

"Okay," Mamma says.

Daddy gets up from the railing and offers Mrs. Caruso an arm.

I watch the three of them walk slowly across the wraparound porch to the back steps and then down into Mamma's garden. "You sure these are peach trees?" Mrs. Caruso asks.

"I'm never sure of anything. Come on. I'll show you my pathetic watermelons and you can tell me they look like summer squash."

Mrs. Caruso erupts into laughter.

They disappear into the garden behind us. I close my eyes and push my feet into the railing so the hammock swings back and forth. I love this day. Today I am the birthday queen. There is a new girl moving into the neighborhood. Mamma made me a green-peach pie, and the four people I love the most in the whole wide world are here to celebrate my birthday.

Suddenly Tess stalks from her place on the steps to the hammock, where I am rocking back and forth. She grabs my face with icy fingers and pulls me up so I am looking at her white, terrified face.

"What's wrong?" I ask.

"You've done it, Lizzie. You've really done it this time."

"What did I do?" My heart is beating hard.

"The wish," says Tess. She lets go of my cheeks, but I can still feel the imprint of her fingers on my skin. "The wish you made. That every day of the next year will be just as good as this day. You said it out loud, Lizzie."

Now she is holding herself. Her arms are so skinny you can see the bones beneath the skin.

"It comes true whether you say it out loud or not," I tell her.

"No," whispers Tess. Her voice is low and hollow, as if she has fallen into a hole and is suddenly talking to me from ten feet under the earth.

"If you say a wish out loud, the opposite happens."

She leaves my side and walks into the empty house.

The screen door slams.

AVE MARIA

Holy Mother full of grace
Push the chocolate in her face
If the statue starts to cry
Feed the Virgin pumpkin pie.

AVE MARIA

One week later, the Amodeos move in. We ride our Pink Lady bicycles down the cracked road to see what kind of people they are. We watch them lug a statue of the Virgin Mary down the pine needle path to the cottage. The Virgin is heavy. You can tell because it takes two big boys to put her in the right place, and they keep wiping sweat off their shiny foreheads and making sounds like old stairs creaking. They finally put her down in the rock garden, right next to some old lobster traps and a pile of rope. A woman crosses herself. She takes the boys in her arms and kisses them like they just saved her life.

They unload furniture all morning, heaving it over roots and rocks and down the steps to the sighing house. They carry lamps and couches and chairs and tables, and pictures and mirrors and boxes of stuff that couldn't possibly fit inside.

They unload a silver crucifix and a painting of some saint with doves sitting on his shoulders. The kids run all over the place making noise and fighting with one another, but the woman stands right there next to the pile of rope and the statue of the Virgin Mary and watches it all with watery eyes. I think she would have knelt down in the pine needles and hugged that statue for dear life if she could have done it without looking crazy.

Pretty soon we can hear a baby crying for its mamma from inside the house. The woman wipes her hands on her skirt, touches the Virgin Mary's cheek with the back of her index finger, and marches to the house with her skirt in one hand.

Tess and I watch the parade of children and furniture. Mrs. Caruso was right. There is a boatload of kids. Tess keeps count every time a new one emerges. As far as we can tell, there are six of them. There's the baby inside the house with his mamma. There is the oldest boy, almost a man. There are two teenagers, maybe high school age. There's a scruffy black-haired boy in ripped jeans, and a girl who looks like she's my age. She has black patent leather sandals that are so shiny the sun glints right off them. When she comes out of the truck with an armload of stuffed animals, we raise our hands to say *Hey*, and she raises her hand back, before making her way into the house.

"We've got to be friends with her," Tess whispers to me

fiercely, her skinny hands gripping my arm so hard that it hurts.

"Why?"

She is breathing fast the way she sometimes does when her imagination gets fired up. "That statue is starving to death," she says. "She needs chocolate bars. She needs them now. She hasn't had anything to eat but bugs in fifty years. If I give her chocolate, she'll make your birthday wish come true. I am going to feed her a Coconut Crunch bar. It is going to fix everything."

"Statues can't eat," I tell Tess.

Tess glares at me, slack-jawed, like I am the one who said something strange.

"We're never going to get anywhere near that statue unless you become best friends with that girl."

"But, Tess," I say, "you're my best friend."

"You have to do this," says Tess. "It's the only way, don't you see? Or your birthday curse will kill us both. The statue can save us, Lizzie." Then she looks into my eyes and it is like a fire burning. I can't look away and I can't say no.

The girl comes out and sits down on the curb next to us. Tess gives me a poke in the arm and I clear my throat.

"I'm Lizzie Cohen," I tell her, my voice coming out all breathy, "and this is my sister, Tess. We live back there on the hill."

"Hi," says the girl. "I'm Isabella Amodeo. We just moved here."

"I know," I tell her. "We've been watching. There aren't any other kids on this street. We never have anyone to play with. Who is your teacher going to be?"

"Miss Stephanie," says Isabella.

"Me too," I say. "She's supposed to be really nice. Do you have a bike? If you want, you can come riding with us later. There's a place by the bridge we like to go."

"I don't have a bike," says Isabella.

Isabella's brothers rush past us and back into the truck where they knock against things and make loud clanging noises before struggling back out, each one with his own cardboard box. The boys jostle one another with their elbows and try to make one another drop things. The scruffy one with the long black hair tries to bow when he sees Tess, but he almost drops his box and the other boys just laugh at him.

Isabella says, "The oldest is Anthony. He works on the lobster boat now that Daddy's gone. Remember that big storm last year? That's what took him. Joey's the baby, he's inside with Mamma. Marco and Robert are in high school. And the ugly one is Niccolo. He's my twin. I'm the only girl."

"Sorry," I say. It seems like the right thing to say, but really I am thinking about what life would be like if I had all those brothers and this girl had Tess.

Tess keeps poking me in the back with her thumb. I know

she wants me to ask about that statue, but I can't think of a way to do it. Tess puts her hand on my shoulder. Her fingers feel like claws.

"Hey," I say to Isabella, "that's a neat statue over there. Can we see it?"

Isabella laughs. "That's the Blessed Virgin," she says. "Haven't you seen a Blessed Virgin before?"

"We're Jewish," I tell her. "We never get to see Christian things up close."

Isabella shrugs and brings us into the rock garden. We sit on the pile of rope and look at the statue. The Virgin Mary poses inside her blue seashell shrine with her hands open to either side of her body. Her head is bent just a little. Her eyes are focused downward. She has a calm, serene smile. She doesn't look starving to me. She just looks tired.

Tess kneels in the pine needles beside the statue.

I look behind my shoulder to make sure Mamma can't see us. If she knew that Tess was kneeling in front of the Virgin Mary she would probably keel over and die. I find myself moving behind my sister like a screen, protecting her from whatever she is about to do.

Tess takes a chocolate bar out of her pocket.

She reaches out quick as a wink and pushes the chocolate bar onto the serene, smiling mouth of the Virgin Mary. She pushes it all over the peaceful face and makes lapping yum-yum sounds the way our mamma used to do when she fed us with baby spoons. Tess doesn't care that Isabella Amodeo is staring at her with her red mouth gaping open in an O. Tess keeps making yum-yum sounds and pushing the melty chocolate bar into the Virgin Mary's wise, impassive face.

"You should stop that before Jesus or my mamma sees you," Isabella warns.

"Don't worry," says Tess, her voice all proud like a new mommy who's gotten her baby to eat her first bowl of oatmeal. "She's just having a snack. She'll feel better now. Jesus will thank us for doing this, believe me."

"We're not supposed to play with the statue," says Isabella doubtfully as she watches Tess smushing chocolate into the Virgin's face. "Mamma says if I am disrespectful I might go to hell. I don't know you, but I don't think you would want to go to hell. You'd better stop. What did you say your name was?"

Tess wipes her chocolaty hands on her blue jeans. The Virgin Mary's face is brown and gooey and she has chocolate stains on her blue robes. She smiles calmly down at the ground, evidently full and satisfied. "I'm Tess. And I'm really sorry if this goes against your religion, but I am not going to hell for giving chocolate to a starving lady. Plus I'm Jewish. We're the chosen people. We don't have to worry about hell. God's already made his decision about us."

"That's not true," says Isabella Amodeo, sounding like she's going to cry. "Anyone can go to hell. Even Jews."

Tess looks worried. She folds the candy wrapper into a

perfect triangle and puts it into the back pocket of her jeans. Then she smiles. "I'm sorry, Isabella, I know you're new around here and everything, and I want to be nice to you, but you're wrong about this. Jews go to heaven no matter what. Besides, I don't need to worry about things like that. I am immortal."

And with that, Tess takes my hand, turns away from Isabella Amodeo and the chocolaty Virgin, pivots on her heel, and drags me back up the path to where our Pink Lady bicycles are waiting for us.

Isabella Amodeo sits in the rock garden next to the statue of the Virgin Mary. I can't be sure, but I think she crosses herself as we ride away.

ENDYMION

When she teaches something she loves, Ms. Lozano is high-strung and nervous like a whippet with jittery legs. She gets so excited that her hands shake and she has to hold her wrist to keep her book steady. She flits around the room with a tattered copy of Keats in one hand and her shaking wrist in the other, overpronouncing each word and savoring vowel sounds as if they were dipped in honey. She wears Indian skirts that swish when she walks, and that she smooths over her bare skinny knees when she perches for a moment on the edge of a low bookshelf or the top of a desk. Then she's off to flutter again, like a colorful, bizarre bird. Sometimes I don't listen to the poetry at all, I'm so distracted by her movement and the sight of her. I wonder about what kind of coffee she drinks in the morning, and whether all that movement comes from having one cup more than she should—or if she hides a pack of unfiltered cigarettes in her rose-quilted teacher bag and takes a drag between classes with a shaking hand. She is reading poetry to us, and Keats's words tremble from her lips like spiderwebs.

> *A thing of beauty is a joy for ever:*
> *Its loveliness increases; it will never*
> *Pass into nothingness; but still will keep*
> *A bower quiet for us, and a sleep*
> *Full of sweet dreams, and health, and quiet breathing.*
> *Therefore, on every morrow, are we wreathing*
> *A flowery band to bind us to the earth.*

She always glances at me, or leans toward my desk when she reads because she knows I get it. It's true. I do understand the poems. Keats is obsessed with death. He is always worrying over art and decay and whether things we create will stay around on earth or eventually crumble like a Roman column, or rot into the ground like a corpse, the skin sliding off the bones, and then the bones themselves sifting away like chalk. Ms. Lozano sometimes tells me that I have a poetic soul, which is ironic, because I've never written a decent poem in my life. My soul understands and analyzes and thinks and criticizes but it does not and never has created anything beautiful. Tess was the beautiful soul. Tess was the poet. So I guess it's fitting that even dead, Tess is the one who's impressing the teachers.

I didn't originally plan on handing in Tess's poems each week. Not in the beginning. But I was looking at the Pegasus Journal so closely in my weekly sessions with Kaplan that I began to memorize Tess's words, and once I memorized them it was easy to pass them off as my own. And then once I started getting decent grades, it was hard to stop. I became addicted to the guilt. The strange thrill of doing something so morbid, so off-color, and so completely wrong.

I do love reading the comments Ms. Lozano scrawls across Tess's poems. Ms. Lozano has strange handwriting that curves and slants and loops above and below the line like vines. Her comments are effusive, filled with exclamation points and underlined words. Sometimes she uses a single word made expressive by a certain slant or curl in the letters. For instance, when she likes a metaphor or simile, she writes *Ahhhhh* in the margin and her letters sigh downward so that I imagine her taking a long sip of coffee and then sinking into a comfortable chair. This is when she generally tells me that I have a *poet's soul* or an *outstanding musical ear*, or that my poems have a *gentle, lilting lyricism*. Of course, Ms. Lozano has no idea that the student she really loves has, as Keats might say, passed into nothingness. The irony is almost too delicious to bear.

In my notebook I write *"A thing of beauty is a joy for ever . . ."* and then I cover the page with question marks. I know Tess's poems are beautiful. That's why I hand them in. But despite what Keats says, I take no joy in them. I feel somehow compelled to go back to them every week, one at a time, to handwrite them over and over in my own notebook, and then finally to type them and even sometimes to read them in front of the class as if they were my own. But they do not give me "sweet dreams" or "quiet breathing," as Keats suggests. They give me nightmares. When I read Tess's poems I feel like I am choking. And yet here they are, all typed out in my binder with Ms. Lozano's effusive handwriting looped around the lines like roses. I know what they are. They are evidence. They are a condemnation. They are an umbilical cord to my guilt.

When class is over, we all file past Ms. Lozano's desk to hand in our drafts. I take out the poem "Queen of Toads," the one Tess wrote the day we killed all those hoptoads. My poem has no sketches on it but the memories hide in the white space. Tess's little four-line poem sits by itself in the center of the empty page like a child bending her head in the snow.

I don't notice Isabella's brother Niccolo reaching past me to put his poem into the folder. He jostles my elbow and I stumble forward. Tess's poem floats down onto the green linoleum tile. Niccolo picks it up for me and then stands there reading the words to himself, his lips moving, measuring the metrical patterns with his fingers on the page. I haven't really looked at him since the funeral. He is still scruffy and he has the same ridiculous smile he had when we were kids. "This is really good," he says. "You signed your name Lizard Cohen instead of Lizzie.

That suits you. You have become a bit reptilian. Don't run away. You always rush out of here so fast, we never get to talk. It's been a long time, Lizzie. How are you these days?"

"I'm late for class," I mutter. I take the poem and hastily place it into the folder and then rush past the rows of chairs and out of the classroom. Niccolo keeps pace with me all the way to the door and down the green linoleum hallway, looking at me sideways with a sort of half smile as though he finds the very sight of me hysterical, which irritates me even more. I pick up my pace.

"You've changed, haven't you?" Niccolo is jogging to keep up with me, his battered green army bag swinging from his shoulder. "The whole arrogant black-turtleneck-and-*don't-talk-to-me-or-I'll-kill-myself* thing. You want people to be scared to talk to you? If I didn't know you, I guess I'd probably stay away. You look like you want to hit me. Want to take a shot?" He grins and gives me his chin.

I ignore him and storm over to my locker. *Right to seven, left two times to twenty-three, right again to nine.* Seven . . . twenty-three . . . nine. I pull hard. It's jammed. I punch the door with my fist and repeat the combination. Seven . . . twenty-three . . . nine. I pull harder. I rattle the lock and pound on the gray metal with the palms of my hands, then with my fists. I rest my forehead against the cool face of my locker and grumble obscenities to myself, but Niccolo is still there yapping away as if nothing unusual is happening. I pound my locker door with my head.

"I really liked your poem," he tells me, moving one of my arms so that he can peer into my eyes. "There's something childlike about it. I find that intriguing considering how you look these days." He motions up and down my body and I know that he is talking about my black turtleneck, my ripped jeans, and my combat boots. I don't care. People see what they want to see. I give the lock another shake and the clatter echoes down the corridor.

Niccolo touches my elbow. "Do you want me to try that? I've always been good at locks. Isabella hates it, but it does come in handy."

I don't answer him. It seems that he's not looking for an answer. He takes my hand like a dancer and double-spins me away from my locker. Then he puts his ear to the door and begins moving the dial very slowly, caressing it with long fingers. "It's all in the clicks," he tells me. "If you get really close you can tell how to do it. You have to slow down. Be really gentle. Listen to the give. Then all you have to do is . . ." He lifts the lock and the door swings open, a dark square hole. He runs his hand across the frame. I just stand there with my heart pounding.

My locker is a mess. There are binders and books stacked on top of each other. There are half-finished packs of chips and crushed empty Dunkin' Donuts coffee cups. There are containers of breath mints. There are unfinished homework assignments. There are piles of tests with red-pen scrawls across them, hurried notes from worried teachers trying to save my soul. They write things like *See me* and *Please, Lizzie, come for extra help* and *Let's talk about this.* Some teachers are too disgusted to write anything at all. They just scratch their C or D on the top of the page and underline it three or four times to remind me that they mean it. And of course, there is always the F for failure. F for failing falling festering failure. F for fault. F for forgotten.

Suddenly I feel naked. Niccolo stands there looking into my open locker as if he has just unbuttoned my shirt. He breathes in all those horrendous grades and unfinished assignments. He breathes in the half-empty packs of chips and the crushed Dunkin' Donuts coffee cups. He stands there and looks and doesn't move away. He doesn't know what I know. There are secrets in this hole. There is a ghost looking down at both of us: a girl with wild red hair. In the corner of the locker, on the top shelf, wrapped in an old wool sweater, Tess's Pegasus Journal arches its spine like a cat. It purrs and pulses in the dark. It hisses its vicious warning.

I slam the locker door.

It sounds like a punctuation mark. Like a period at the end of a sentence.

COCONUT CRUNCH

Chocolate is for mortals
With their cravings and their curves
With their fleshy flabby bellies
And their butt cheeks and their rumps.
When they walk their butt cheeks jiggle
And they drool when dinner's served
Then they gorge themselves and belch
And swallow steak in sticky clumps.

How could they know mortality
Is all wrapped up in food?
The more they eat the faster
They approach their final hour.
With their breath all sour and salty
And their nails and teeth unglued
And with clumps of hair unfastened
Every time they take a shower.

I eat the mist from tide pools
Drink the wind from ragged rocks
Instead of flesh and fat
I feed on periwinkle stones
A cup of roaring laughter
When the waves crash over docks
And instead of fins and fish cakes
I have moonbeams on my bones.

COCONUT CRUNCH

Every morning, Mamma puts Tess on the scale to see if she's gained any weight. Tess stands still in her panties and undershirt with her hands on her hips, looking anywhere but down where the numbers spin and spin and stop on seventy-five. Everything about Tess has bumps and angles. She's a human staircase. Her ribs, her spine, her cheekbones, her knees. If she hasn't gained anything or, God forbid, if she has lost a pound, Mamma brings Tess down to the kitchen and spoon-feeds Cream of Wheat into her open mouth. This morning, the sun casts triangles of light across the wooden floorboards and Tess sits on the yellow stepladder with her skinny hands folded across bare knees. Mamma has a bowl of Cream of Wheat and butter. She spoons it in. Tess opens her mouth like a baby bird and swallows.

Mamma doesn't talk. She just slips in spoonfuls of Cream

of Wheat. Mamma's eyes are quiet and serious. They are filled with something I can't name. Sometimes Mamma touches Tess while she feeds her. She traces a line across her jaw and down her tiny rosebud fingers. She makes it look like she's touching Tess to remind her that Mamma loves her no matter how small she is, but I know why she really does it. She is measuring. She is feeling the skin and the bones underneath. She is saying to herself, *The last time I did this there was more. The last time I did this, the bones didn't show. Oh, my poor little baby. Oh, what are we going to do with you?*

Dr. Swan smiles and says that Mamma shouldn't worry. When Tess gets hungry enough she'll eat. He's known Tess and me since we were newborn babies and he says if Mamma makes a big deal of this, Tess is gonna fight back in her own way sure enough, just like she's always done. "After all," says Dr. Swan in his comforting doctor voice, "everyone knows that Tess Cohen likes to be dramatic. It's hardwired. Been that way since she was a newborn."

"Let her eat whatever she wants whenever she wants it," Dr. Swan tells Mamma when she breaks down over the examining table, in tears because the scale says seventy-five and Tess's fingers and wrists are as skinny as chopsticks. "If she wants meat loaf give her meat loaf. If she wants chocolate bars, give her chocolate bars."

So Mamma says, "Tell me what you want, Tess, honey." And Tess says, "I want Coconut Crunch." Four words that make Mamma smile like the sun is shining down on us all.

"Well, there you have it," says Dr. Swan, patting Mamma on the shoulder.

After the appointment Mamma goes down to the corner store and buys bags of Coconut Crunch chocolate bars and fills Tess's pockets with them. She puts Coconut Crunch chocolate bars in Tess's jeans and in her underwear drawer, and whenever Tess looks a little pale and tired, Mamma gives her Coconut Crunch.

What Mamma doesn't know is that Tess doesn't eat most of the chocolate bars. She saves them for the Virgin Mary statue. Every morning, Tess tiptoes down the path to Mrs. Amodeo's rock garden, where the Blessed Mother stands waiting in her blue seashell shrine with her hands open to either side of her body, and crams Coconut Crunch chocolate bars into the tight, smiling mouth.

Isabella Amodeo watches Tess feed the Virgin chocolate bars from her bedroom window. She crosses herself so Jesus doesn't come and punish Tess for being disrespectful to the Blessed Mother full of grace. Isabella Amodeo crosses herself: *In the name of the Father and the Son and the Holy Spirit, amen.*

Every morning I take Tess's cold hands and lead her away from the Virgin Mary, away from Isabella Amodeo's house, and back to the road where our bikes are waiting for us. Her fingers are so thin I can feel the bones.

As we walk away, I can hear the front door creak open, and scruffy little Niccolo tiptoes from the house, real quiet so their mamma won't hear. He kneels in front of the statue for a moment, his lips moving in silence. Then he pulls an old red bandanna from the pocket of his overalls. With the care of a painter, he wipes and wipes and wipes her face, her chin, her lips until every stain has vanished and the Virgin is white and pure again. When he sees me watching, he winks.

———

The days go by. August fades into September and school starts. "What's wrong with your sister?" Isabella Amodeo asks that first week at recess. We're swinging in the playground and the chains make a creaking sound when we pump our legs. The wind blows our braids and whistles up beneath our skirts, making us feel like we are flying. The seagulls cry from somewhere down by the harbor. I don't know what to answer so Isabella asks me again. "What's wrong with your sister, Tess?"

What's wrong with my sister?

What's wrong with my sister, Tess?

I pump higher. I'm flying over the chain-link fence, over the houses, the blushing oak trees, over the whole world. I turn into a Pegasus. I spread my gold-dust wings and I leave Isabella Amodeo behind, asking her questions and wondering things I have no answers for. I fly away. I fly far, far away. I let the wind take my words and my thoughts. I let the wind brush its smooth fingers over my cheeks and forehead like Mamma used to do when I was a baby crying too hard and she needed to calm me down. Rocking me. Rocking me back and forth. I fly away and I don't come back until Miss Stephanie comes over and says, "Come on now, Lizzie, it's time to come in. It's time to stop swinging now, Lizzie." She helps me slow the swing and then puts her arm around me and leads me down the concrete path to the fifth-grade classroom.

There are tears streaming down my cheeks and I am hiccuping and coughing and Isabella Amodeo has already gone in for quiet reading and so have all the other boys and girls and I am alone on the path with Miss Stephanie. I can't even remember what Isabella said to me or why my cheeks are burning and covered with tears. All day long I am sad, like someone has hung a thousand sandbags around my neck, and I keep wanting to cry.

"What's wrong, Lizzie, honey?" Miss Stephanie asks me over and over again. But all I can say is I *don't know* and it's true. I don't know what is wrong with her. But for the first time in my life I think it might be something bad.

BLUEBERRIES

Virgin Mother, full of pies
Full of prayers, sins, and lies
Hissing juice through frozen lips
Drizzle drool, the sweetness slips.

BLUEBERRIES

On Sunday after Mass, Isabella's mamma gives our mamma a phone call. She says today she's making blueberry pies, and she wants to know if we want to go with Isabella and Niccolo up to the mountain to pick the last berries of the season. If we pick enough, she'll send us home with our very own blueberry pie all warm and sweet for dessert. She says she sure could use our help. Mamma doesn't hesitate. As soon as she hears about the pie, she pushes us out the door. "Go on, it's the neighborly thing to do. And don't forget to bring back the pie. Hurry now, so they don't leave without you."

Isabella's mamma gives each one of us a pail and tells us to come home with our pails filled to the brim. "You can eat some of them,"—she laughs—"but not all of them. Mind Niccolo. He's apt to eat the whole field before you get home." Niccolo grins and licks his lips. He is a lover of wild blueberries. But

Isabella promises to keep him honest. We set off with our pails banging against our legs, up behind the houses to the blueberry field where everything smells sweet. Pine pitch and cinnamon, and the deep blue smell of blueberries all around.

Niccolo and Tess settle down by some low bushes and get right to picking. Tess makes it into a game. First him, then her. First him, then her. He picks a big one, she picks a big one. He picks a small one, she picks a small one. At first, they make blueberry echoes as the first berries plop down into the pails. *Plip. Plop. Plip. Plop.* But soon they have so many on the bottom of their pails that there is no sound. They are serious about it, using their thumbs and forefingers to pluck the best ones. They are like picking machines with long, mechanical fingers, reaching in and plucking, and the blueberries fall like notes from a harp. "I love the color," says Niccolo, his eyes soft and wistful. "Blueberry blue is the bluest blue there is."

"Blueberry oceans," sings Tess. "Blueberry skies. Blueberry pickers for blueberry pies. I'm going to write a picture book about blueberries."

Niccolo nods emphatically and claps his hands. Tess takes a bow.

"There are too many picture books about blueberries already," says Isabella, putting her hands on her hips. "Come on, Lizzie. Let's go over here."

She takes my hand and marches me over to the bushes high on the hill. We squat down together and get picking. I pick some and eat some, and pick some more and eat some more. Isabella is a perfectionist. She knows how to make them fall right into her pail by touching them with one finger. She finds the ones that are so ripe they are ready to leap from the bush.

I eat the juiciest, roundest blueberries, the ones that make my tongue sing. My pail fills up with tiny ones, sticky ones, overripe and shriveled, blueberries that are less than perfect. "You should pay attention to what you're picking," says Isabella. But I am thinking that Niccolo and Tess are right, and blueberry blue is the bluest blue there is, and every time I put a berry to my lips it is as if I am swallowing a little piece of sky.

Behind me, Niccolo and Tess are still playing games with blueberries. Niccolo kneels down and Tess pitches blueberries into his open mouth. "*Ping!*" shouts Tess, and she takes one from the bush and flicks it from the palm of her hand onto his tongue. He eats it. He eats every one.

"Don't forget to pick some too," Isabella warns. "Mamma needs these for her pies."

Tess grins. "Oh, Isabella," she says, "you are such a mortal."

"You are so weird," mutters Isabella.

"*Ping!*" cries Tess, and she flicks another blueberry into Niccolo's mouth.

I watch them and can't help but smile. I would like to play their game too, but Isabella and I are more serious about our work. Her pail is already almost full, and mine is filling up. The blueberries look good together, little round jewels with

117

perfect crowns, blue gems filling the pail. Roundness against roundness. "Come on, Lizzie," says Isabella, and holds my hand. We move to a new bush where the blueberries are begging to be picked. She shows me how to help them off the bush just by petting their sides and tipping them into the pail. These are the ripest ones so far. They make our fingers smell like autumn. Isabella holds my hand and smiles whenever I get it right.

"You're smart," she says. "You learn fast." I like it when she says things like that.

Then a sound makes me turn around. It is Niccolo's soft voice saying *"Ping!"* and I see something I can barely believe. Tess is kneeling down in the grass with her mouth open. Niccolo pitches a blueberry into her mouth. She swallows it. *"Ping!"* And another and another. She is eating. She is eating one berry after another. Niccolo stands closer so he can get more to go in. He takes handfuls of berries from his pail and tips them into her mouth. She chews and swallows and opens her mouth for more. *"Ping!"* whispers Niccolo, his voice as soft as wind. "There you go, Tess. They're yummy, right? Good for you. Eat them up. Magic berries, Tess. Magic berries." Tess's eyes close. She rises up on her knees so she can be closer to Niccolo's hand. She sniffs and snuffles and eats them right from his open palm like a horse with soft lips. My cousin Marney had a pony once and she used to let us feed him sugar cubes. That pony would stick his white nose into our hands and take the sugar with the softest lips. It felt like our skin was being kissed by clouds. I watch Niccolo feed magic berries to my sister and I think about that pony. I wish it was my hand she was kissing.

"Hey," says Isabella. "You two. Stop it right now. You are wasting berries."

"She's really hungry," says Niccolo.

"She can have her very own pie when Mamma's done."

"But pie isn't magic," says Niccolo. "She only eats magic things. Blueberries have spells inside them. They help her fly."

Tess whinnies and paws the earth. Then she begins galloping around the hill, pretending to fly. She stretches her arms out to either side like moonbeam wings. I wish I could fly with her. I wish I could take a magic blueberry and spread my wings like she does and we could lift into the air together, but nothing feels the same with Isabella by my side. I still remember the words Tess taught me back before summer started, but when I say them they come out all wrong. "*Nardo pardo,*" I whisper. I spread the fingers of my free hand like horse feathers and very gently move them up and down. Nothing happens. Tess trots over to me, her mane and tail tangled from the blueberry bushes. She snorts and tosses her head. Niccolo pats her. "Good girl," he says.

"Oh please," Isabella grumbles. She sounds disgusted.

"I've filled up my pail, Isabella," I tell her. "And you've filled up yours. I think between the two of them, they've probably got another. That's three pails of blueberries. Don't you think that's enough?"

"Well I guess it'll have to be."

Tess turns her back on Isabella. She tosses her head and blows air through her lips. Then she puts her hands on the ground and kicks Isabella in the kneecap with a wild neigh.

Isabella falls over.

I rush over and help to pick her up. Isabella's face is red.

"Are you okay?" I ask.

"No," says Isabella. "I'm not."

We head back down the mountain in silence. Niccolo carries the pails. I put my arms around Isabella so she can lean on me while she walks. She limps a little and walks a little. Her knee isn't really all that hurt. But her feelings sting because Tess kicked her. Because Tess and Niccolo are friends. Because things didn't go as she thought they would. Between us, we have three pails of blueberries. It will make three good pies. And later, after Mrs. Amodeo sends us home, we'll be able to fill our tummies with our very own blueberry pie made from the very last blueberries of the season. Tess won't have any. Niccolo was right. There is nothing magical about pies. But Tess is filled with magic blueberries, and now she is flying down the hill with her arms outstretched, her red hair flowering behind her like fire.

DEEP RIVER

Rock me gently down the stream
Rip my song from parted lips
Hold my breath, a strangled scream
Merrily the rowboat tips.
With this worm, I do thee wed
Clammy lips and open eyes
Rotting on the riverbed
Consummated where she lies.

DEEP RIVER

We start to go down to Isabella and Niccolo's house to catch fish every day after school. We sit on their floating dock with rods and pails filled with night crawlers. Isabella and I do most of the fishing. We sit back-to-back with our lines in the water. Tess is the Mistress of Bait. Her job is to push the point through one blind end of the worm, forcing the astonished body down the shaft. She loops it twice so it doesn't wriggle free. Tess is not ladylike. She rubs dirt and worm blood on the pockets of her jeans and doesn't even mind. She plays with the worms in the bucket of black mud. Sometimes she pulls one from the pail and loops it around her finger like a wedding ring. "Oh, Niccolo," she sings, flexing her tiny wrist and beholding the wriggling jewel on her finger, "I will marry you! Yes I will!" Niccolo flushes so red, he looks like a circus balloon.

Isabella doesn't laugh at Tess's joke. She leans back into my shoulders, and pulls her line up. Then she casts with a sharp flick of her wrist. The quick silvery line sings out across the river. We wait. The wind comes up. Niccolo takes out a harmonica and starts to play "Row, Row, Row Your Boat." Isabella rocks back and forth and I rock with her. I like the way the sun feels shining down on us, and I like the sound of Niccolo's harmonica and the water and the wind, and the feeling of sitting back-to-back.

Isabella takes a deep breath and begins to sing: "Row, row, row your boat / Gently down the stream. / Merrily, merrily, merrily, merrily, / Life is but a dream." And then I start, and then Tess joins in. Pretty soon our voices are louder than the seagulls or the motorboats or the water lapping the sides of the floating dock. "Row, row, row your boat / Gently down the stream. / Merrily, merrily, merrily, merrily, / Life is but a dream." We sound good together.

Niccolo's harmonica sounds like wind through the pine trees. Isabella has a church-choir voice. It's high and pretty and it reminds me of angels. My voice isn't anything special. I can carry a tune though, and I keep my part of the round going, all the while rocking back and forth with Isabella leaning against my shoulders.

When it's Tess's turn, her voice explodes from her belly. Tess sings louder and louder and she kicks her feet into the river so water soaks the floating dock. Pretty soon she drowns out Niccolo's harmonica and Isabella's voice and my voice, until it's just Tess belting "Row, row, row your boat" at the top of her lungs.

"When you sing a round, you're supposed to try to blend," says Isabella. "Tess was way too loud. Tell her, Niccolo. Tell her she was too loud."

Tess is grinning with shining eyes.

"I think you sounded good," whispers Niccolo.

Isabella glares at him and he shrinks away.

"Let's eat something," I say, trying to change the subject. Isabella's mamma packed us a basket of snacks to keep our energy up while we fish. There's a pepperoni and some over-ripe cherry tomatoes and a hard-boiled egg for each of us. I hold my fishing rod between my knees and pop a cherry to-mato into my mouth. The juice runs down my chin.

"You look like a vampire!" Tess shrieks. She flops over my lap and throws back her head with her skinny white neck ex-posed. Her tangled hair trails down onto the dock. She is very dramatic. "Bite my neck," she gurgles in a strange, hollow voice. "Bite my neck and suck my blood." I give her a little bite on the side of her neck. Tess shrieks. Then she makes a swoon-ing sound and pretends to die. Her legs kick and kick and then go stiff. She lets a line of drool seep down the corner of her mouth.

"That's gross," says Isabella. "You shouldn't play like that."

Tess scrambles beside me and kisses me on the cheek.

"Lizzie and I always play like this," she says, her voice gone hot from the challenge. "If you are going to hang around with us, you'll have to get used to the way we do things. Right, Lizzie?" She puts her skinny arm around my shoulders.

I don't say anything.

"We don't have to get used to anything," says Isabella. "If you want to hang around with me and Niccolo, you'll have to stop playing crazy games. Our mother would be mad if she knew you were pretending to be a vampire. You're going to need to stop all that when you are around us, or don't come back at all." Isabella's voice rises as she speaks and rings in my ears even after her final syllable has ended. The sound of her words bounces from the pine trees and the boats and the waves and the buoys chiming in the distance. We all look at one another, not saying anything.

"That's okay," says Tess, finally. "I don't really like you. Come on, Lizzie. I changed my mind. I don't want you to be best friends with this girl. I want you to be my best friend again. Say goodbye." She takes one of my hands and pulls.

I get ready to follow her off the floating dock, but Isabella takes my other hand and pulls me back down. She curls her arm around my shoulders. "Tess Cohen," she says, staring right into my sister's eyes like a bull, "if you don't calm down, there's no more Virgin Mary for you. I'll tell my mamma that you've been sneaking into the rock garden in the morning to feed chocolate bars to the Blessed Virgin and that the only

126

reason she doesn't know is because Niccolo creeps down after you every day and cleans it all up with our daddy's old handkerchief, and she'll tell your mamma and your mamma will tell your rabbi, and then you'll be in trouble with the Jews. Is that what you want?"

Tess stops dead in her tracks. She considers this. "No," she says. "I wouldn't want that."

"Well then, behave yourself," Isabella says sweetly, "and sit down. I want to try the round again."

Niccolo grins. He blows a musical gust into his harmonica.

I take a deep breath.

Tess slumps down on the dock.

Isabella and I settle into our comfy fishing position, back-to-back, and I can feel the smoothness of her hair on my neck and shoulders. When she speaks, her voice vibrates all across my back. "Now, I want you to try to blend, okay, Tess? You don't have to be an opera singer. Just listen to my voice and Lizzie's voice and Niccolo's harmonica and keep yourself under control. No more crazy stuff. You'll see. It's much better that way."

"Much better," says Niccolo.

"Okay, Isabella," says Tess. "I'll do whatever you say."

This time when we sing the round, our voices blend into one beautiful circle, Isabella's church voice, Niccolo's harmonica like wind through the pine trees, my good-enough voice, and Tess's onetime powerhouse voice gone somehow all soft and wispy and strange. Tess sits by herself on the corner of the floating dock. Her skinny legs dangle into the water. They cut the current like fins. She puts one finger down and traces circles in the river until her pale, distorted reflection looks back at us, eyes blank, face white, lips barely open.

Row, row, row your boat
Gently down the stream.
Merrily, merrily, merrily, merrily,
Life is but a dream.

I've never heard Tess sing so softly. I have to strain my ears to hear her, and even then, her voice is more like a suggestion, a shadow of a voice, like a line in the Pegasus Journal that's been rubbed out so many times you can barely see it. Tess looks hard at my face with murderous eyes. She blows me a kiss from her place on the corner of the dock. Then she lets her body drop into the water. Her red hair billows out behind her like seaweed. Her shirt lifts. I can see the milky white of her skin. She bows her head and sinks to the bottom.

We stop singing.

"What's she doing?" asks Isabella.

"She's pretending to drown," I tell her.

"That's stupid. Why would anyone do that?"

"She's mad at us."

Niccolo looks frantic.

128

"Jump in and get her out," says Isabella.

"She's pretending," I assure them. "Just wait."

Niccolo grabs my hand, his eyes wide and pleading.

"Get her out, Lizzie," says Isabella.

I don't move. I am watching her sneakers kick. They stir up pebbles and mud and they cloud the river so we can't see her face.

One one thousand. Two one thousand. Three one thousand.

Tess stops kicking.

Four one thousand. Five one thousand.

The current turns her face up below the surface. Her eyes are open.

"Get her out, Lizzie! Get her out!" Isabella screams.

I don't move.

Niccolo crosses himself and scrambles to the edge of the dock, but then there is an enormous splash and the sound of coughing. Tess's soaking body breaches the surface. She gulps air into her lungs. She opens her beautiful mouth and gasps and gasps the wonderful air back down to her body, spluttering and coughing and barking the water out of her lungs. She staggers for shore, making her way out of the river and onto the rocky beach, her red hair plastered to her back in tendrils, her clothes dripping darkness onto the cold stones.

Shivering, Tess turns around and grins at us.

She pulls a sopping Coconut Crunch bar out of the pocket of her jeans and heads back to the path that leads to the falling-down cottage and the rock garden and the statue of the Blessed Mother. Niccolo pulls his daddy's old bandanna out of the pocket of his jeans. He follows her silently. We can hear Tess laughing and screeching, "Row, row, row your boat" at the top of her lungs, all the way up the pine needle path to the statue of the Virgin Mary, *Gently down the stream,* who is waiting with ears that will never hear and eyes that will never see, *Merrily, merrily, merrily, merrily,* and a mouth that will never taste the chocolate my drowned sister who rose from the dead to walk again will smear back and forth and back and forth across the pale motionless lips. Niccolo will hide behind the pile of rope and lobster traps. He will wait until she is finished, after I have taken her hand and led her home. Only then will he kneel in front of the statue. He will use his father's old red handkerchief to wipe all our sins away. *Life is but a dream.*

FUNERAL SHROUD

Here is something most people don't know about me. I don't wear black because I'm a rebel. I wear it because I want to disappear. There are other kids who wear black, but for them it's just a fashion statement. Their black includes various accessories like open-fingered gloves that lace to the elbow, fishnet stockings, and extra piercings in their ears.

Don't get me wrong. I don't have anything against these kids. And I do partake in the occasional studded collar. But my black isn't just a fashion statement. It's a necessity. I wear black because wearing a color would make me a hypocrite and a liar. When I wear color, I feel like everyone knows I'm faking it. Black might not tell the whole story, but it's a millimeter closer to the truth.

"And maybe, just maybe, you wear it because you want

people to worry about you," says Kaplan one Wednesday. It is January. There is snow outside the window, and the space heater in his office emits a continuous white hum that makes me want to close my eyes and sleep. Kaplan is wearing green wool socks. He is leaning back in his swivel chair regarding me, half smiling. "You want them to take one look at all that black and worry about how sad and lonely and bitter you must be. Poor, poor Lizzie."

"That's ridiculous," I tell him. "Why would I want people to worry about me?"

"You tell me."

"I hate it when I ask you a question and you answer me by asking the same question back."

"Hey," says Kaplan, grinning, "that's why I get paid the big bucks. If you think about it, you might learn something about yourself. I'll ask your fine question again. Why would you want people to worry about you?"

"I know what you want me to say," I tell him, staring above my head at the wooden horse that circles silently on its white frayed strings.

"What's that?"

"You want me to say that as long as people are worrying about me, then they're still thinking about Tess. And as long as they're thinking about Tess, it's like she isn't really gone. Right? Same reason I hand in her poetry." I smile at him. "Denial is not just a river in Egypt, you know."

"So by turning in her poetry you don't have to face the reality that she has died and that she is not coming back."

I grin. "*Yah, Herr Doktor.* And as long as *ze* patient *eez* handing in her dead sister's poetry, she does not *haf* to deal with her own feelings of grief *und* shame." I say this in a melodramatic, thick German accent. Then I hold out my hand for Kaplan to give me a high five but he doesn't.

"Lizzie," says Kaplan, "this is serious. Did you listen to what you just said?"

"I always listen to what I say," I tell him, still smiling. "I may be neurotic, but I am not deaf."

"As long as you keep wearing black, people are going to think about Tess. Every time they see you, they will be reminded. *That poor girl. It's been years. And she's still in mourning?* Every time they talk to you, every time they see you, they are reminded of the death. They don't have any other way to know who you are. You, my dear, are a walking funeral."

"That's very poetic."

"Thank you," says Kaplan. "It's also true."

"Well, I'll go after school and buy myself a pink dress. Will that make you happy?"

"Will it make *you* happy?"

"That's really infuriating, Kaplan. I ask you if it will make you happy. You ask me if it will make me happy. A never-ending loop. So I'm asking you. If I show up next Wednesday wearing a frilly pink dress, will you, Kaplan, jump up on this desk and do the happy dance? Will you prance around your office like a crazy fool, hooting and giggling and slapping yourself silly? You tell me."

Kaplan shakes his head and smiles. "You are insufferable," he says.

It is a compliment.

I feel myself blushing. And for some reason that moment of happiness is almost unbearable. I reach up above my head and touch the wooden horse with one finger. It turns silently on its strings. Its red eyes glint in the sunlight. They are Tess's eyes.

"I don't want to talk about this anymore," I say.

"Okay," says Kaplan. "What do you want to talk about instead?"

"I want to look through the Pegasus Journal and decide which poem I'm going to hand in to Ms. Lozano on Friday. Do you want to help me pick?"

Kaplan smiles his lopsided smile. "Doesn't that make me an accomplice to your life of crime?"

It's a joke but it rings in the air like truth and we both listen to his words bounce around his office in stunned and embarrassed silence.

"Don't worry, Kaplan," I say. "My crimes started long before I started coming to see you."

Kaplan nods and makes a face that means he's sorry about how that came out. "Show me the Pegasus Journal," he says softly. "Tell me about a page near the end when things started getting bad."

Above my head, the wooden horse turns silently on its strings. Its red eyes catch the light filtered through the icicles hanging down outside the office window.

I open the Pegasus Journal.

There is a sketch of two little girls in a rowboat. Their eyes are bleeding.

First Betrayal

Fairies dance through midnight dark
Glistening wing tips, spirits spark
Thinnest arm, extend and arc
Point their toes, the brine-wolf's bark.

Fairy circlets, crowns of green
Seaweed pearls and silken sheen
Gowns of azure tangerine
Fan thine arms, to pose and preen.

If I could I'd spider-spin
Webs of silver, moonbeam-thin
And I'd lure the fairies in
Make them dance and bid them grin.

Then when church bells chime the hour
Kiss their cheeks and snuff their power.

First Betrayal

Isabella's rowboat is big enough for four people but it goes faster with two, so we leave Niccolo and Tess on the dock and row out to the middle of the river alone. September is coming to a close. The tips of the oak trees are starting to turn orange and there is a chill on the river. Tess and Niccolo get smaller and smaller. The high seagull-song of Niccolo's harmonica floats away until I can hardly hear it. Soon I can barely make out Tess's slumped form, the motion of her feet moving back and forth in the water. It's peaceful in the middle of the river. Every once in a while, a crow or gull flies above us making its noise. I can see the fishermen's cottages all up and down the bank, and the now-abandoned summer cottages looking out over the river with their new glass windows and their wooden decks, left like the empty husks of cicadas on the banks until next year.

Isabella takes one oar and I take the other and we row right into the cove by the salt marsh where sea grass grows so high it looks like green waves. We lift our oars into the hull and let the rowboat drift into the marsh grass until it stops in the reeds. Then we lie down across the wooden seats and breathe in the sun and the crisp air and the smell of salt. From somewhere far away, I can almost hear the sound of Niccolo's harmonica floating along on the wind. It feels strange to have Tess so far away. I can't hear her making up stories. I can't see her eyes blazing. I know she's still there on the dock, I can feel it, but somehow with the salt water lapping the sides of the rowboat and the wind blowing on our faces I could almost forget.

Then Isabella starts to sing "hey, ho, nobody home," and after she sings it three times through, I've pretty much learned the melody, so I close my eyes and join her when it comes around again. Our two voices lift above the rowboat and float over the water. Our two voices high-five each other in the air above our heads and then they find a seagull looking for herring. They grasp the seagull's wings with invisible fingers and they soar with him out over the fishermen's cottages and the empty summer cottages. Our voices look down on the river and the rowboat and the two girls singing together, and they laugh.

This is real live magic. And Tess isn't even here. I made it myself. I am so happy with my spell that tears well up in my eyes. I hope that Isabella's eyes are closed too so that she doesn't think I'm crying because I'm sad. We sing and sing and sing.

Hey, ho, nobody home
No meat no drink no money have I none
Still I will be very merry
Hey, ho, nobody home.

"You're my best friend," says Isabella.

I think I might break open. "Me too," I whisper.

Isabella reaches for my hand and pulls me up. Our knees are touching.

"Were you crying?"

"No," I say, wiping the tears away with the back of my hand. "Hay fever."

Isabella smiles suddenly. She puts the oar down into the water and flicks me.

I flick her back.

If you let your oar down just a little bit from the oarlock and then, quick, quick, pull in toward the boat, you can flick water on the person across from you. The more you practice, the better you get. We become very good at making water spray onto each other's heads. Before long, our hair glistens with water and our eyelashes are dripping.

It's my idea to finish flicking and row back to the middle of the river again. I don't ask her if it's okay, I just start rowing and Isabella follows my lead. The reeds swoosh across the bottom of the rowboat and when we emerge from the green stalks, the sun seems even brighter and the water sparkles. "There are fairies in the water," I tell her in my best mysterious voice.

"Oh, really?" says Isabella. "Fairies in the water."

"Yes," I say, grinning. I stand up on the seat of the rowboat and put my arms out to either side like wings. I begin to flap.

"Don't tip the boat." Isabella giggles.

"Fairies, fairies, we are coming down to visit you!"

Isabella is giggling so hard she has to hold on to the sides of the boat to keep her balance. "They're not in the sky, you big goof! They're in the water! You're flapping like a seagull! You should be pretending to swim!"

I stop flapping. "You're right!" My voice is serious. I step out of my jeans and sweatshirt. Now I am standing there on the seat of the rowboat, shivering in my panties and undershirt. The cold air blows across my skin. I know that I am smiling like a fool but I don't care. It feels good to do magic this far away from Tess. "Come on, Princess Isabella. We must return to the fairy realm. Risest thou up and jumpest thou into the cool, refreshing deep with me."

"You're crazy," says Isabella. But she strips down to her underclothes too.

We look at the cold, green water. Then we look at each other. She comes up slowly, first squatting on the seat with her hands on either side of the boat and then straightening little by little until we are facing each other, shivering. Isabella's silver cross glints in the sunlight. The rowboat wobbles and totters every time we move. We collect ourselves with our arms out to the sides. We breathe slowly in and out.

"We shouldn't be doing this," says Isabella. "It's going to be really freezing."

"I know." I grin. "But we have magic. It will keep us warm."

"Count one two three and then we'll both dive in at the same time."

"Okay." I giggle. "I'll do anything to help us get back to our rightful throne. Even if it's dangerous and cold. Listen to me count and then we'll dive in together. Only then will the spell be complete. One. Two. Three."

We dive in at the same moment. She goes off one side and I go off the other. The water is so cold it numbs our skin, but we don't care. We look for seaweed under water. I find two slick strings of green pearls. When we bob up to the surface, I put one in her hair and one in my own and now we are both fairy princesses and any time we come back to this spot on the river we will be royalty.

It isn't easy to get back into a rowboat from the water, but if you have the right kind of magic, you can do anything. You have to get one leg over, and then pull yourselves up at the same time. One. Two. Three. Go. Our seaweed crowns are still on our heads and our teeth are chattering, but we are happy. We struggle back into our jeans and sweatshirts. We row in silence closer and closer to the muddy banks where the tide is starting to go out.

The closer we come to the floating dock, the more clearly I can see Tess. She is standing next to Niccolo, waiting for me, frowning. As soon as she spots the rowboat, she begins pacing along the edge of the dock. She reaches out to pull me in, even before Isabella drops the anchor and ties the rowboat to the metal post at the corner of the dock. I climb out of the rowboat first but I do not take Tess's hand. Instead, I put out my hand for Isabella and she takes it. I fix her seaweed crown and smile at her. She puts her hands to either side and flaps like a seagull. We collapse into each other, damp and shivering under our clothes, laughing at our perfect secret.

"What's so funny?" asks Tess.

"Nothing," I say.

"Nothing you would understand," says Isabella. We can't stop giggling.

"You have seaweed in your hair," says Tess.

"Yes, I know," Isabella says, smiling. "Lizzie gave it to me."

Niccolo shrugs. He climbs up the ramp where seagulls have smashed their catches. He starts chucking dried crab bodies into the water. They float out on the tide: bodies, pincers, jointed legs, shell fragments, the feathery insides—a parade of orange corpses bobbing up and down on the ripples. Then Niccolo finds the grandmamma of all crab bodies, a huge red shell with all its legs and its two front claws intact. Niccolo winds up like a baseball pitcher and lets it go right out over the river. It hits a rock that juts out at low tide. The grandmamma crab shatters into pieces. The smell of rotten meat. The sound of an egg cracking open.

ANGEL

I lean back in the armchair and watch the snow fall against the window. Everything outside is gray. The sky is gray. The courtyard is gray. Down by the harbor, the ocean and the fishing boats are gray. The relentless, freezing February wind comes up from the ocean like a ghost. From somewhere far off, I can hear a seagull screaming.

I leaf through the pages of the Pegasus Journal one by one, looking for something to move us forward. Kaplan is patient. He doesn't rush me. He just sits back in his chair and waits for me to speak. Here is a page covered in eyeballs with fishhooks jabbed through pupils. I flip that one over. Here is a sketch of two little girls sitting in a rowboat. The rowboat is on fire, and the girls' faces are melting. I flip that one over too. Finally I stop on a picture that makes me catch my breath. It is an angel with magnificent feathery wings that extend to either side of the page. Tess has detailed every feather so you can see the separate filaments, and she has done something with light and shadow so that it looks like the sun is glinting off the page.

At first glance, the picture is beautiful. Alarming in its detail and its texture. But then, when you let your eye travel inward, away from the magnificent wings, you can see that the angel's body is emaciated and sunken like the body of a corpse, as if the wings are the only part of the angel that is alive. The bones show through the flesh. You can see the tendons, the muscles, the veins. The face is little more than a skull with skin stretched across the bones.

"Kaplan," I say.

"Yes, Lizzie."

"Do Jews believe in heaven?"

Kaplan looks at me. "I don't know," he says.

"I wish I believed in heaven," I tell him. "It would make things easier."

"Would it?" says Kaplan.

"Isabella believes in heaven. That's why she always wears that stupid silver cross. I think tomorrow I'll go to the jewelry store to buy myself a silver cross. I'll wear it around my neck every day, just like Isabella. What do you think of that, Kaplan? Would that make you happy? It would? Okay. That does it. I'm sick of all this Moses and Merlin stuff. I'm converting to Christianity. Halle-bloody-lujah."

Kaplan doesn't say anything. He is watching me very closely.

I sigh and look back down at the sketch. "Do you think this is what she looks like under the ground? Right now, if I dug her up and looked?"

He raises his eyebrows.

"Do you think after five years there would still be any skin? Or would it all be bones by now? I bet the skin would be gone. Even when she was alive, there was not much more to her than bones. I think about that sometimes. About opening her coffin and looking inside. I wonder if I would recognize her. I bet it would be easier recognizing someone bony like Tess than a different kid who was fat and fleshy when he was alive. I bet I'd look down at all those bones and say Yup, that's my sister. But the fat kid, no way. No one would recognize him. Not even his very own mother." I start laughing. I laugh so hard that tears begin to roll down my cheeks. "I'm cracking myself up," I say. I reach for a tissue and wipe away the tears.

"Yeah," says Kaplan. "You're a real hoot. Listen, Lizzie. There's a reason you stopped on this picture. What is it? Don't tell me you wanted to discuss the decomposition of corpses. The relative decline of fat versus skinny bodies. Go back to the beginning. What did you ask me when you first found this picture? It was important. And then you went off track."

"I asked you if I should go to the jewelry store and buy myself a cross," I say, still grinning.

"No," says Kaplan. "That wasn't it."

148

I trace the angel's wings with the tip of my finger.

"I asked you if Jews believe in heaven."

"Yes. That's right. Now why did you ask me that?"

I look down at the sketch of the angel. Suddenly, I feel unspeakably sad.

"Because I don't know," I tell him. "I've never known what to believe. Isabella knew the words to all the prayers. She was so sure about how it all worked."

"And what about you?" Kaplan asks.

"Me?"

"Yes, Lizzie Cohen. What about you?"

"I don't know. When I was little I thought Moses and Merlin were the same person. Whenever I saw my grandma saying a prayer over the bread or the wine or the candles, I thought she was casting a magic spell."

"Well," says Kaplan, "what are you going to do about that?"

"I'm gonna go get me some old-time religion! Hoo-ey!" I holler like a hillbilly and slap my knee. Then when I see that Kaplan isn't smiling, I compose myself. "No really, Kaplan. I'm probably not going to do anything about it. I kind of enjoy confusion, if you haven't noticed."

"Lizzie," says Kaplan, "you are the one who asked me whether Jews believe in heaven. I'll change the question slightly and ask it back to you. Now listen carefully. And answer me without making it into a joke. Do you believe in heaven, Lizzie?"

I look down at the angel corpse one last time and this time I stop smiling.

"No," I say finally. "I don't believe in heaven. But I'll tell you what I know for sure. There definitely is such a thing as hell. And you know what? You don't even need to die to get there."

LOW TIDE

Palm the velvet mud at noon
Carve the clam beds, cleave the moon
Blue crabs crouch 'neath craggy stones
Egrets bleach their weathered bones.

Eels through sea grass whip and slither
Plovers preen and shorelines shiver
Sunken docks and broken boats
Tilt their heads and slit their throats.

LOW TIDE

On Saturday, Mamma and Daddy bring us down to the floating dock to watch low tide take the river. Mamma packed lunch in a wicker basket. It is October. The sky is clear and blue, and the oak trees on the far side of the river have turned a brilliant red. We are all in jeans and wool sweaters. Tess sits on the dock with her Pegasus Journal, her red head bent furiously over the page, shoulders hunched and tense. I glance over. She has drawn a girl's face with the eyes and mouth stapled shut.

The sun shines down and makes the mud smell like the bottom of a dog's paw. At first it looks like nothing's moving, but if you look hard, you can see that even the brown snails move, a millionth of an inch at a time. There is movement in the clam holes, bubbles rising to the surface. A stream of water shoots up from the mud like a tongue pushing spit through clenched teeth.

"Time for lunch, everybody."

Mamma unwraps odds and ends from the basket: cucumber pickles, blackberries, Italian bread, prosciutto, smoked salmon, different kinds of cheese. She arranges it all on the blanket and we take what we want. I make a sandwich with smoked salmon, blackberries, and brie, a combination that makes Daddy laugh. He scruffles my head with one bear paw.

"A girl after my own heart." He smiles.

I take a bite and settle back against the ramp.

"What are you going to have, Tess?" Mamma asks.

"I'm not hungry," says Tess.

Mamma comes up behind Tess and peers over her shoulder at the sketch of the girl's face. "My goodness," she says. "Such a disturbing image. Put the book down for a minute." Her voice sounds tight. She lifts the Pegasus Journal from Tess's hands, closes it, and lays it down beside her. Then she puts her hands on Tess's curled back. "Honey. You have to eat something. Now look. I brought all your favorite foods. There's even a Coconut Crunch bar. See?" She reaches into the back of the picnic basket and pulls out the candy bar. Tess stares at it.

"Listen, kiddo," Daddy says in a soothing voice. "When I was your age, I was picky too. Didn't like much of anything. Bet you can't believe it lookin' at me now, but I used to be a skinny-minny just like you. Here. Have a bite of this scali bread."

Tess looks down at her lap. Daddy pulls off a piece of Italian bread and pops it in his mouth. "Mmm-mmm. Fresh from Silviano's. You don't know what you're missing, Tess. This here is good stuff." He tears at it wolfishly.

I take another bite of my salmon, blackberry, and brie.

Mamma kneels next to Tess and strokes her tiny hands. She smooths out Tess's fingers on the knees of her jeans. Then she begins to work her fingers across Tess's wrists, rubbing the bones and then kissing the skin. I take another bite of my sandwich. My hands are shaking.

Daddy reaches for the carton of blackberries. He pops a handful into his mouth and then wipes his lips and beard with the back of his hand. "Delicious." He grins. "There's nothing like blackberries. Have some, Tess. When you were a little girl, you loved blackberries. Do you remember?"

Tess frowns and purses her lips.

Mamma holds out a berry and Tess slaps it away.

The wind blows cold on the river. There is the sound of a seagull calling.

Tess begins to cry. Softly at first, and then louder.

"Stop crying," Mamma shouts, her own voice breaking.

Daddy puts his hand on her shoulder. "Calm down, Lillian. Remember what Dr. Swan told you."

"Don't tell me to calm down. I don't care what Dr. Swan

says. Look at her, Marty. Look at her wrists. Tess. You listen to me. I am still your mother. I don't care how old you get. I will not let you starve yourself. Do you hear me?" She grabs the carton of blackberries out of Daddy's hands and pushes a blackberry up to Tess's lips. Tess clamps her jaw shut. Mamma smears the blackberry against Tess's mouth. Purple juice runs down her chin.

"Eat," Mamma pleads.

Tess slaps Mamma's hand away. Mamma cringes, cradling her hand, tears streaming down her face.

Then Daddy grabs Tess's shoulders, pulls her close, and holds her. "Eat, goddamn it! You think you're stronger than me? I've got news for you. You're tiny. I can hold you down with one arm. Now eat!"

"Please, Tess." Mamma is trying to make her voice sound rational. Normal. "One berry. Just one."

I have finished my sandwich. It sits at the bottom of my stomach like a rock.

Daddy forces handfuls of blackberries against Tess's closed mouth. She struggles against Daddy's hold, but pretty soon one berry goes in. Nobody moves. Tess tastes the blackberry. She rolls it on her tongue. She swallows. Her eyes close. Her body relaxes. In a little while Daddy lets go of her. Mamma crawls back across the dock and sits herself down next to her daughter, who is hugging her knees and moaning softly. Mamma wraps her arms around Tess. She places another blackberry against Tess's lips and Tess takes it, more gently this time. She swallows another and another. She snatches the container and pops them into her mouth one after another, tears and blackberry juice streaming down her face. Mamma kisses her hair, her eyes, her cheeks. She rocks her back and forth.

My face is burning. For the first time in my life, I hate her. I hate her. I close my eyes and make a horrible wish.

A white seagull flies by. He drops a crab onto the dock. The body shatters.

"Mamma," I whisper.

She pulls Tess across her lap and cradles her.

"My poor baby," she murmurs. "My poor little baby girl."

It was a horrible wish. Such a horrible wish.

"Mamma, can I go to Isabella's house?"

Daddy puts his arm around me. "Of course you can go," he says. He puts two fingers under my chin and tilts my face up to his. "Everything is going to be okay now," he tells me.

I leave them on the dock, Mamma rocking Tess while she eats and Daddy looking on with tears in his eyes. I climb back up the ramp, cross the dock, and then take the path through the pine trees to Isabella's house.

Behind me, the sound of low tide drifts off into the distance.

PASSOVER

Even though Mamma and Daddy are Jewish and both grandmas and grandpas were Jewish, and even though the three of us always eat a big Passover meal with the candles on the table, obligatory brisket and matzo ball soup, we are definitely not what I would call a religious family, especially since Tess died. While it's true that we have never bought, nor have we ever been tempted to buy, a Christmas tree, and while we are probably the only people on the river who don't take Communion, or cross ourselves to ward away evil, or eat fish on Friday and early suppers after church on Sunday, and even though it's true that Mamma and Daddy like a good bagel when they can get it, we are nothing like Mamma's cousin Max, who is by far the most Jewish person I have ever met. Compared to Max, we are complete heathens. It's true. I don't believe in God any more than I believe in magic. And the last time I heard anyone speak Hebrew was at Tess's funeral.

Max wears a prayer shawl tucked into his pants, and he covers his head with a yarmulke every single waking day, not just at weddings and funerals like Daddy. Whenever he visits, Max makes us remind him which window in our house faces east so that when he wakes up in the morning— before he shaves or brushes his teeth or even speaks to any of us—he can go stand at the east window and mumble-sing Hebrew words I can't understand, with tunes I can never remember, holding his tiny gold prayer book, and bowing back and forth, closing his eyes and bending his knees and making me feel empty inside like the old coal stove rusting out in the backyard, all covered with pine needles.

When I ask him what he is doing, he looks sad and says I should know what he is doing, especially since tonight is the first night of Passover. If my parents had bothered to send me to Hebrew school I would have known. He is thanking God for allowing him to rise up in the morning to face another day. He is reminding himself that there are more important things to think about than the matzo and cream cheese or lox and whitefish that Mamma has set out for breakfast in the kitchen downstairs. Sometimes Mamma gets annoyed at his proclamations. She calls him Mr. Holier than Thou, and clenches her teeth when he tells her later that afternoon that no self-respecting Jew would let her fifteen-year-old daughter dress like a vampire, all in black.

"You think I look like a vampire?" I ask him, fascinated and a little pleased by the idea, since I often feel like one of the undead, a tormented soul wandering the earth.

"She doesn't look like a vampire, Max," says Mamma sharply, while she chops the hard-boiled eggs and the chicken livers on the cutting board so that the cleaver striking the wood sounds like a woodsman's ax. And then she turns to me and says in a softer voice, "You don't look like a vampire, Lizzie. Really. Don't listen to him. You look perfectly fine."

Mamma shakes in salt and pepper and goes back to chopping. The cleaver strikes the wooden board and the sound echoes inside the kitchen. *Chop. Chop. Chop.* The silence settles on our shoulders like dust.

My mother looks up and gives Max a weak smile. Maybe she is sorry for snapping at him, but she is too tired to apologize. "I'm glad you've come to lead our seder, Max. It's been a long time."

"I'm glad you invited me. But I hope Marty won't feel like I'm taking his role away from him. He is the man of the house, after all."

Mamma's back stiffens. "I don't think you have to worry about it. Marty hasn't led a seder in years."

There is a strange silence. Then Mamma goes back to

chopping. The cleaver resounds. *Chop. Chop. Chop.* The house smells like chicken fat and onions and soup boiling on the stove. The kitchen table is already set for dinner tonight. There is a lace tablecloth that used to belong to Grandma Ruth. There are candlesticks and wineglasses and matching plates. We work together in the kitchen. Chopping, stirring, getting ready. The table waits for us in the middle. Four empty chairs.

"When is Marty coming home, Lillian?" Max asks in a low voice.

"I don't know," says Mamma.

"I hope he comes back in time for the seder," I say.

"Me too," says Mamma. "But let's not count on it."

At sunset, Daddy is still not home, so we sit down together without him—Mamma, Max, and me at the kitchen table and one empty chair for Daddy. No one says anything about it. Max strikes a match and says the blessing over the candles. He circles his hands above the flame and closes his eyes. We watch him, silently.

Baruch atah Adonai
Eloheinu melech ha'olam,
Asher kideshanu bemitzvotav
Vetzivanu lehadlich ner shel yom tov.

That's when we hear the click of the door and Daddy stalks in. A stranger. The kitchen is not used to his presence. It feels too small for him, all the walls, the counters, the refrigerator, leaning in. He walks to his place at the empty chair, lowers himself down, and runs a hand through his hair. Max smiles at him. It is a weak smile that is filled with more than friendliness. Daddy has not shaved his beard and he is still wearing his work clothes. Mamma does not look at him. She keeps her eyes on the candles. Two tiny flames, flickering in the dim light.

CONFESSION

Bless me, Father, I have sinned
Mamma left my dress unpinned
Tore my skirt and made me curse
Forbidden fruit into my purse.
Whip me so I won't forget
Blight me till I squirm and fret
Send down lightning, boils, and lice
Thorny toads and naked mice
Then when night bleeds into day
Strike me down and make me pray.

CONFESSION

I kneel in Isabella's closet. She takes my hand and leads me into her darkened room.

"Tell me what to do."

Isabella has made a confessional by hanging patchwork quilts from each corner of her four-poster bed that takes up most of the space in her room. The quilts are fastened to each bed knob with rubber bands. She plays a tape recording of Benedictine monks singing in Latin and her bedroom sounds like a cathedral. The men's voices join together, rising to the top of the ceiling like angels. There are candles flickering from her bookshelves. Isabella turns off the lights in her bedroom and plugs in the Holy Cross night-light. It glows blue in the corner of her room. She lifts one corner of the quilt and climbs into her bed. She closes the curtain. I hear the bedsprings moving. The sheets rustle.

"Come inside, my daughter."

I lift the curtain and climb up. I kneel on a pillow. Isabella's made a screen out of an old white nightgown. I can't see her but I know she's in there. I can hear her breathing.

"Well?" comes Isabella's voice from behind the nightgown.

"Well what?"

"Cross yourself and then say *In the name of the Father and the Son and the Holy Spirit.*"

"I don't know how."

"How to cross yourself?"

"Yeah."

There is a silence and then: "Head, chest, left, and then right."

I cross myself with shaking hands. "Bless me, Father, for I have sinned."

"Now tell me how long it has been since your last confession."

"I've never been to confession. I told you. I'm Jewish. We only confess once a year on Yom Kippur."

"Say it anyway," says Isabella from behind the white nightgown.

"Okay. In the name of the Father and the Son and the Holy Spirit, I have never been to Confession before because I am Jewish. Now what?"

"Now you tell me your sins and I listen to you. Say the hardest sin first. And you have to really be sorry or else I can't absolve you."

"What does that mean, *you can't absolve me?*"

"It means you'll suffer for your sin forever and then you'll burn in hell."

I swallow.

"Go on, my child. Tell me what's wrong. There's no sin so great that our savior, Jesus Christ, can't forgive you."

My heart is racing. I hold the corner of Isabella's pillow between my thumb and forefinger and roll it back and forth on the balls of my fingers. It doesn't help. My insides are twisted like fishing bait writhing in a metal bucket. "I did something terrible, Father. Something that can never be excused."

"What is that, my child?"

"I have a sister."

"Yes. Go on."

"Well, lately it hasn't been so easy to get along."

There is silence from the other side of the nightgown.

"And I've started getting kind of angry at her."

I can hear Isabella sigh. "Lizzie, this is supposed to be a real sin. Being angry at Tess isn't that bad. I get angry at Niccolo all the time. Don't you have something worse than that?"

"It is worse," I say miserably.

I can hear Isabella reposition herself on the other side of the screen. When she speaks next she is the priest again, her voice peaceful and mild and wiser than mine. "In what way is it worse, my child?"

"Today I was so angry at her I made a wish that she would die."

Isabella huffs. "That's normal, Lizzie. Give me something good."

"It's not normal," I snap. "You don't understand. It wasn't just a quick wish, the kind you make when you've had a fight and the thought flashes across your mind for a second. This was a real wish. Like when you wish on a star. Or when you wish really hard before blowing out your birthday candles. Mamma and Daddy were worried about how skinny she is. Poor Tess. So so skinny. Skinny wrists. Skinny knees. What are we going to do? They tried to feed her but she kept her mouth clamped shut. And I thought, *I wish you would just go ahead and starve yourself to death.* And I looked right at her and thought the wish words as hard as I could. *Tess,* I said in my mind, *I wish you would just die. Just die already, would you? We've all had enough.* Now do you see why I needed to make a confession? I did something unforgivable."

"Nothing is unforgivable, my child. Jesus Christ will forgive you if you are truly sorry in your heart. Are you truly sorry?"

I can't answer right away. I am thinking about it.

"My child, I can't absolve you unless you've examined your conscience and have fully resolved not to ever make such a wish again. Otherwise this isn't a true confession. So I'll ask my question again. Are you really truly sorry?"

I think about Tess on the dock, rocking back on her heels,

shoveling blackberries into her mouth, her lips stained purple, my parents watching her with tears in their eyes.

"Yes," I whisper. "I am really truly sorry."

"Then you must promise to give your sister another chance. You must never wish for anything bad to happen to her again. From now on, every night before you go to sleep, you must pray to Jesus Christ to make her well. If you pray hard enough, Jesus will listen to you. He will grant your wish."

"I don't think the Jewish God does that," I tell her.

"What does the Jewish God do?"

"Well, he pretty much waits and watches. And sometimes he sends a lightning bolt."

"That's why you need to pray to Jesus. Jesus likes to get involved. Go ahead. Pray to him."

"Now? Out loud?"

"Yes. Kneel and put your hands together and pray for Tess's soul right this second. There's no time to lose. Come on, Lizzie, before something bad happens."

I kneel and put my hands together. It feels strange. Once a year, on High Holidays, Mamma and Daddy go to synagogue. They close their eyes and sway forward and back on their heels, and the synagogue is filled with everyone's song at once. Sometimes they put their arms around each other and sometimes they touch their hearts with their prayer books. They don't know the words to all the prayers, but they move their lips and make the right kinds of sounds. Ever since Grandpa

Morris died, Mamma prays with tears in her eyes. Almost all Jewish prayers start out the same way, so I begin with the only words I know in Hebrew. "*Baruch atah Adonai, Eloheinu melech ha'olam.*"

"Excuse me. That's a Jewish prayer," says Isabella from behind the curtain.

"Just the beginning of one."

"Pray the rest in English."

I take a breath. "Blessed art thou, Jesus Christ, Lord of the Universe, who has sanctified us and commanded us to pray for our sisters. I ask thy forgiveness for thinking such bad things. I don't really want Tess to die. I just get so worried about her sometimes. And I get tired of worrying. Please help my sister, Tess, eat more chocolate bars so she doesn't die of being too skinny. Her ribs all stick out and her face looks like a skull and my parents are really worried. Help her get fatter, oh King of the Universe. Just ten more pounds so Mamma can stop weighing her. And please help me be a better sister. Help me watch over her and protect her like a good sister should. In the name of Abraham and Isaac and Rachel and Leah and the Father and the Son and the Holy Spirit." I cross myself again. Head, chest, left, right. "Amen," I say.

"Now we leave the confessional," says Isabella in her own voice.

Isabella pulls down the patchwork confessional, first the white nightgown, then the four walls. The quilts fall to the floor like rainbows. We fold them together corner by corner and end by end. I find the tape player and turn off the Benedictine monks. All the sounds seep away from the cathedral and her ceiling is just a bedroom ceiling again. We blow out the votive candles, one by one. There is the smell of smoke and wax. Isabella looks at me with wide eyes. She unplugs the blue Holy Cross night-light from her wall. Then she crosses herself and closes her eyes. "Amen," she whispers.

POETRY DOUBLES

When Ms. Lozano tries to teach something brand-new, and she wants the class to get inspired by it, her voice becomes breathless and she begins to sound like one of those nighttime telephone escorts, the kind that show up on television around three in the morning when you can't fall asleep, and you're just clicking through channels looking for something to make your brain go numb. I don't know if anyone else in our class has noticed this similarity, but I made the connection the last time I had insomnia. I was clicking through all the late-night television networks and there on channel 27 was one of these telephone escorts talking all breathless, and suddenly I realized she sounded exactly like Lozano. All I could think about was Ms. Lozano on late-night TV with a copy of Walt Whitman in one hand and a pink telephone in the other. *Hi*, she breathes in my imaginary world, *this is Teresa*

Lozano, and I want to talk dirty to you. Do you like romantic poetry? A glass of wine by the fire? A reading of "Ode on a Grecian Urn"? Call me at 877-54-GIRLS. You won't forget it.

Ever since then, whenever Ms. Lozano gets breathless, I want to fall on the floor laughing, because all I can think of is our teacher on some raunchy late-night infomercial. I try to stifle my laughter and what comes out instead is an evil, twisted smile, which Ms. Lozano always mistakes for enthusiasm. This misunderstanding drives her to move closer to me, and to use her most dramatic gestures. She nods in my direction, which makes me want to laugh even harder. The evil smile widens, and the cycle continues until Ms. Lozano is practically leaping on top of my desk, and I am holding back tears, with my teeth clenched and my fingernails digging into my arms to stop myself from losing control.

Today, Ms. Lozano is introducing a new idea she calls Poetry Doubles. She weaves up and down the rows, and reads from the assignment sheet.

Introduction to Poetry
Friday, April 1

Poetry Doubles

Over the next month, this class will practice the art of collaboration. You and your partner will be responsible for creating an anthology that reflects the best of your work this term. Using extensive conferences and peer comments, you must revise all of your previous poems until they are realized to the best of your ability. You also must create one new piece that reflects the skills you have mastered.

She looks up from the assignment sheet and scans our faces. Then she takes a dramatic breath. "Do you see, kids? It's not about inspiration. It is about perspiration." She spots my evil smile and floats over to my desk. "Right, Lizzie? Sweat. Tears. It's about pushing hard. Again. Again. Trying the same thing from new angles. Lifting each other when it's good. Bringing our partner down ever so gently when it's not. Can you get into that? I mean, can you feel what I'm saying?"

I nod at her and then look around the room to see if anyone else appreciates the sexual innuendo, but my fellow classmates are expressionless, watching Ms. Lozano float around, taking notes in their poetry binders like serious little scholar-robots. They have all missed the double entendre. I guess Principal Palazzola is right. I am smarter than these clowns. Ten extra points for Lizzie Cohen, who was paying attention last year in freshman English when we learned about the double entendre.

"You and your partner will experiment," Ms. Lozano goes on. "Take risks. Try new things you never thought were possible. I promise you, if you practice enough times, that powerful creative muscle that lies dormant when you're not working will become stronger, more piercing and more potent." She demonstrates this by pumping her fist.

The other students in the rows around me are scribbling diligent notes filled with Roman numerals and lowercase letters. I crane my neck to see how this raunchy diatribe could possibly translate into outline form. The kid sitting next to me has a page that looks like this:

Poetry Doubles

    I.   Perspiration not inspiration
    II. Doing it together helps
         a. Pushing hard
         b. New angles
         c. Raise them up and come down gentle
    III. Benefits
         a. Try new things
         b. Creative muscle
         c. Piercing and potent

My smile gets wider.

"Of course, we'll need a fair way for you to choose your partners, so I've put your names in a hat. I'll come around now. Reach in and announce who your partner is. Lizzie Cohen, I'm coming to you first. You look so happy you are ready to burst." She floats over to my desk with a huge floppy velvet hat she must have bought at some Renaissance fair from a guy dressed up in tights and a cape. Some man named Frank who calls himself Sir Wolverine three weekends each year, who talks in fake medieval English and bows to the middle-aged women who don't look nearly as good as they think they do in chain-mail bikinis. Ms. Lozano's floppy hat provides the finishing touch to her telephone-escort outfit. I can see it now. The floppy velvet hat with the peacock feather, the black sequined negligee, the high-heeled studded boots.

"Here's the hat, Lizzie."

"Thanks," I splutter.

"Go ahead, Lizzie. Choose your partner."

"Don't take all day," somebody mumbles behind me.

I put my hand into the hat and twirl my fingers across the folded index cards that contain the names of my classmates. Suddenly it hits me. Someone is going to be reading and critiquing Tess's poetry. If I am going to pass this project, I will either have to write my own poems or I will have to revise Tess's. I can't write. If I'm going to pass this project, I'll have to destroy the only thing I have left of Tess. I'm going to kill her again. Murder. Cold-blooded, premeditated murder. Suddenly I am imagining Ms. Lozano in her phone-date outfit ripping pages out of my sister's notebook with a steak knife. Words and sketches fall to the classroom floor like seagull feathers.

I can't do this. I can't do this.

My heart pounds in my ears and the classroom swirls around me.

Ms. Lozano's bright, expectant face zooms close to me like some kind of strange tropical bird.

I can see the kids in all the rows with their binders open, leaning in to watch me, the clock on the wall ticking deafening drumbeats into the classroom, the posters of romantic poets—Coleridge, Keats, Wordsworth—swirling like old white ghosts on a merry-go-round, all around the room.

Now Ms. Lozano and the kids in their seats are rooting for me. They chant my name. "Lizzie. Lizzie. Lizzie." I hold my breath. Then Tess's voice comes clear and cold into the classroom. The voice of an eleven-year-old girl. *I'll never let you go, Lizzie. No matter what happens to me, I'll never ever let you go.*

My fingers stop moving.

"She's waiting for inspiration," Ms. Lozano tells the class. "Don't wait for it, Lizzie. Remember, this project is about perspiration, not inspiration. Commit to it. Pull a card."

Inside the hat I curl my hand into a fist. The white edges of an index card bite into the palm of my hand. I gasp.

I'll never let you go, Lizzie. No matter what happens to me, I'll never ever let you go.

"I'm sorry," I whisper.

"Come on, Lizzie," says Ms. Lozano, "either you do it right now or I'll do it for you."

I close my eyes and breathe.

I draw my hand out of the hat and look at the name on the index card.

"Who is it?" sings Ms. Lozano, her voice triumphant. "Who will be Lizzie Cohen's partner? Let's go. Nice and loud now so we all can hear."

I have no voice.

Ms. Lozano rips the crumpled index card from my hand and smiles.

"Niccolo Amodeo!" she cries. "Lizzie Cohen, meet your poetry double. Mr. Amodeo, I would say you are a very lucky young man. Lizzie is a talented poet. You are going to learn a lot from her."

Niccolo looks straight at me. He smiles.

I put my head down on my desk.

———

At the end of the day, when I open my locker, there is a note hanging on the inside of the door.

Friday, April 1

My Dear Lizard,

Meet me on your floating dock tomorrow, Saturday, at low tide. I want to start working on this right away. I am really looking forward to making poetry with you. And, yes, I am aware of the double entendre.

Yours,
Niccolo

I rip the note in half. I rip it again and again until the linoleum floor is feathered with tiny triangles of paper. I slam my locker shut. Tomorrow, when low tide takes the river, I will be as far away from the floating dock as I can get. I will not look down at the river to see the egrets gather by the water's edge, or the head of a boy I once knew looking out across the muddy banks, waiting for me. I will never meet him there. And even though it's April and I know the project is not due until May, I know with a dead certainty that Niccolo and I will never make beautiful poetry together, no matter what the innuendo. I do not have any poetry of my own. And I will not revise Tess's words. I will not take their perfect lines and question and analyze and ruin what is special about them. Niccolo will sit at low tide without me, watching the sun reflect golden off the mudflats.

KAPLAN

Kaplan is not handsome in the traditional sense. When you look at him, you don't immediately think about movie star hunks, the kind with rock-hard abdominals and to-die-for hair. But there is something about him that gets to me. I'm sure he would call this *transference*, or some other psychobabble. I'm sure if I decided to reveal to him, during one of our Wednesday sessions, that sometimes I find him somewhat attractive, he would tell me it is all just part of the therapeutic process, and it's perfectly normal, et cetera. Who cares? It's not like I'm going to stalk him or anything. But I have to admit, I think about him when I'm not in the chair. Sometimes, just going about my normal day I find myself wondering what Kaplan would think. Sometimes I catch myself shrugging away Mamma's hand when she tries to pet my arm, or I catch myself snapping at Daddy, and I imagine what Kaplan would say.

Do you ever wonder why you do that, Lizzie? Are you paying attention to what you just said? And then I can wait the three or four or five days left before I'm going to see him again, and I know I'll be all right.

This is precisely what happened last week when Ms. Lozano announced that Niccolo Amodeo was going to be my poetry double. I put my head down on the desk and I thought, *Oh shit. What is Kaplan going to think about this?* And then, when I walked out of the room with Niccolo striding after me—*Hey, Lizard. Wait up*, down the hallway to my locker, *Lizard, Lizard Cohen. Stop for a minute. Hey, I want to talk to you*, and I stopped and turned and got on my tippy toes, and put my face right next to his and screamed like some kind of crazy, undead vampire banshee looking for lunch—I wondered how I would describe this to Kaplan. I imagined his face, his thinning hair back in a ponytail, his long, beaky nose, and his eyes filled with that "unconditional positive regard" that all shrinks are supposed to feel for their clients, which is nothing at all like real love, but let's face it, it's good enough when it comes to me and my pathetic issues. I imagined the words he might use to calm me. *It's going to be okay, Lizzie. You've got to believe me. I'm going to help you through this.*

———

Today, instead of talking with Kaplan about Poetry Doubles, I am paging through the Pegasus Journal, looking for pictures that Tess drew of herself. Here is one that isn't so bad. Her eyes are closed, and there is a glowing, shimmery white light shining from the middle of her forehead like some kind of psychic searchlight. She looks peaceful here, relaxed in the river, smiling. And here is another one, rushed, scratchy, detailing one open eye, a nose, a mouth bent in a Cupid's bow. She always liked to make a highlight in the pupil so it looked like light was shining from above.

"You know," Kaplan says, touching my elbow lightly, "Ms. Lozano mentioned your Poetry Doubles project to me. It wouldn't hurt you to give Niccolo a chance and write some of your own poetry. What's the worst that could happen? You end up writing something worthwhile? He gives you some feedback on your actual words? You tell your teacher the truth. Would that be so terrible?"

I scowl sideways at him. "Kaplan," I say, "I don't want to talk about this. Okay? In fact, I have just made the decision. I am not going to take part in this project. I take the F. There. Now please change the subject."

"You choose the F? Even though you know how important it is that you pass this class? Now why would you make such a ridiculous choice? Think about this, Lizzie."

I put one black combat boot up on the coffee table and then the other. "It is just not my cup of tea," I tell him. A slight breeze blows through his open window. It ruffles the pages of the Pegasus Journal. Here is a self-portrait that makes me shiver. She is so skinny, she is almost skeletal. A huge winged toad crouches on her back, and she is bent over so you can see her spine, the fan of her ribs, her pelvis curling like a saddle on a horse. The toad sits on her back and seethes. Its tongue flicks out of its mouth like a snake.

"This will go on your transcript, do you realize that, Lizzie?"

"Stop nagging me about it, okay, Kaplan? Jeez. I love you, but you're starting to sound like my mother. It is just not my cup of tea, Jeeves. Period. Put that in your pipe and smoke it."

Kaplan grins at me. "Lizzie," he says. He likes me even when I'm difficult.

"Yes, Jeeves."

"Tell me the real reason you are refusing to do this project."

"Hmmm," I say, "could *eet* be *zat ze* patient prefers to hand in *ze* poetry of her dead sister? Could it be that *eef* she wrote her own poetry, she would *haf* to come to terms with *ze* tragic death? *Yah*, I do *theenk* so."

Kaplan is not smiling. "You have so much going for you, Lizzie. Too bad you are choosing to ruin your life."

"*Yah.* Too bad."

I flip my hair into my eyes and go back to the pages of the Pegasus Journal. Here is a picture of Tess nailed up to a cross with her hands stretched out to either side. Her neck is limp. She is so emaciated in this picture that her naked body does not even look like the body of a girl. I can see every rib. I can see the outline of her shoulder blades and her collarbone, the ridges in her skull.

"She was so hungry," I whisper. And then I realize I have spoken out loud.

"Hungry?" says Kaplan.

"She was always so hungry I could hear her stomach rumbling all day long. It was just part of the sound she made, this creaky gurgling hungry sound deep down in her belly. But she refused to eat. If you saw her right now, and you didn't know anything about her, if she walked by you on the street, you would think she was dying of AIDS or cancer or some other horrible disease."

"Anorexia is a disease. And people do die of it."

"I know," I tell him, "but this was different. People with anorexia have a messed-up view of their body, right? Skinny girls who think they're fat end up starving themselves. Calorie counting. Binge and purge. That kind of thing. With Tess it had nothing to do with wanting to look like a Barbie doll. It was rebellion. Eating was something that mortals did. Tess did not believe that she was mortal. She was going to live forever. She didn't need food to survive."

"That's ironic," says Dr. Kaplan gravely.

"Ironic!" I crow. "Good use of the literary term, Kaplan. You must have done well in English class. *What is irony, class, does anyone know? Anyone?* Little Sammy Kaplan in the front row is raising his hand. Hair back in a ponytail even then. *I know, I know, call on me, teacher!* Irony is when there are two sisters. One believes she is mortal and one believes she is not. The one that believes she is mortal lives until she is ninety. The one who believes she is not dies before her twelfth birthday. Her casket is so tiny, when they carry it to the graveyard it looks like they are burying a toddler. That, dear teacher, is irony." I laugh. Hard. Tears well up in my eyes and roll down my cheeks. I slap my knees and wipe the tears away. "Oh, that is so funny."

"Are you laughing or crying?"

"I'm laughing," I tell him. "It's the best joke I've heard in my life."

"It's not funny. There's nothing funny about what you've been through. Listen, Lizzie. If you want to cry in my office, it's okay. Lots of people cry in here. People who have a lot less to cry about than you come in here and bawl their eyes out. Go ahead. Let it out, Lizzie."

I wipe my eyes. "Thanks for the permission, *Herr Doktor*, but I would rather laugh, thank you very much. Think about it, Kaplan, the whole thing is absurd. Here's my mother, completely focused on her so-called eating disorder. Weighing her. Spoon-feeding her. Measuring her arms and legs. We worried all the time. Every single moment. When really the eating was the least of her problems. It's hysterical."

"The eating issue was one of the problems." Kaplan sighs. "Your sister had a whole slew of problems, I think. But the eating disorder was more of a symptom than a disease. Do you follow me here? It was part of her delusional world. Flying horses drink moonbeams, not lemonade. Selkies dive into the water and leave their human skins on the shore. And you, the doting sister, you were always in the middle of everything, Lizzie."

He looks at me with eyes filled with sympathy and I feel my face flush. My eyes well up again. I breathe it away. I refuse to cry. I didn't cry at the funeral and I sure as hell am not going to start crying now. I clench my fists. My fingernails cut into the palms of my hands. I shake my head, no.

"You were only ten years old, Lizzie. And she was everything to you."

I take my feet off the coffee table and stare up at the wooden horse. It hangs motionless, one hoof curled to its belly, its head at an angle.

"I should have known," I say. "When she started with the Virgin Mary, I should have known things were going to get bad."

"How could you have known? When you were around Tess, you were half-crazy yourself."

"Crazy is a very general word, Kaplan," I scold him. "And it's a wee bit offensive, don't you think? Especially coming from a man in the mental health profession. You might as well say she was bonkers. Loony tunes. Coo-coo for coconuts. One sandwich short of a picnic. One root beer short of a six-pack.

One slice short of a pizza. The lights are on, but nobody's home!" I slap my knee. *Ba dump bump!*

But Kaplan isn't smiling. His eyes are serious and he leans forward to look right in my eyes.

"I would say she was psychotic," says Kaplan softly. "It's rare in children, but not unheard of. I think if Tess were to walk into my office right now, presenting the way you have described, with all her belief in magic and transformation, I would probably try treating her with antipsychotic drugs and therapy, but when that didn't work, Lizzie, I would have recommended that she be hospitalized before she hurt herself or you. Your parents chose to keep her home. That was a mistake."

"She was only eleven years old."

"It doesn't matter. She needed to be hospitalized and she wasn't."

"That's harsh," I say.

"The truth often is."

"But maybe it's not the truth. She said she could fly. She said she could turn invisible. She said Merlin taught her spells. Maybe that was true."

"Delusions," says Kaplan.

"What if you're wrong," I whisper.

"I'm not," says Kaplan, his face sad.

"But you might be." I try to swallow the lump in my throat, but I can't. "What if all that stuff was actually real, and we were the crazy ones. What if Tess was just a different kind of person from the rest of us? Something new. Something beautiful and new that had never been alive until Tess, and will never exist on this earth again."

Dr. Kaplan sighs. "If that were true, we would be living in a fantasy novel. But this is real life, Lizzie. There is no such thing as magic. You know that. You have always known that."

I reach up above my head and touch the hoof of the wooden horse so it rotates slowly on its strings.

Its red-jeweled eye catches the sunlight cascading in from the window. The mouth of the wooden horse opens. The ears flick forward.

I can hear Tess's laughter. A sound like bells. She would be seventeen years old now, but it is the voice of an eleven-year-old girl that fills the tiny office, a sound like a million butterfly wings beating the air at once.

I'll never let you go, Lizzie.

"Lizzie," says Kaplan.

No matter what happens to me, I'll never ever let you go.

LOCKER NOTES

Monday, April 11

Dear Lizard,

I hope you don't mind that I'm leaving you these notes in your locker, but you've left me no other way to communicate with you. In class you look right past me. You dodge out of the way when you see me in the hall. When I call your house, you hang up before I can speak.

There are less than three weeks left until our poetry project is due. I know we aren't friends anymore, and I know you would rather not be partners with me, but I really want to do this. Please meet me on my dock at the end of the day. I'll bring blueberries. (Do you remember the blueberries?) And poetry, of course.

Niccolo

Tuesday, April 12

Dear Lizard,

I sat on my dock for an hour and waited for you. I saw you come down the road and then turn to take the path up to your house. You didn't even look down here to see if I was still waiting. We used to fish from my dock. Do you remember? Tess would bait the hooks, and you and Isabella would pull up stripers one after another. I still had my harmonica then. The silver one that my daddy gave me before he passed away.

If you give me a chance, I can show you that I understand more than you know. Think about it. And give me a sign in Lozano's class if you are ready to meet with me. Just a thumbs-up will be fine. I'll know what you mean.

Niccolo

P.S. You should clean out your locker sometime. It's a mess.

Wednesday, April 13

Dear Lizard,

Please don't be angry. I found Tess's Pegasus Journal
wrapped up in your old sweater. Back behind your binders
on the top shelf. I knew the whole time those poems were
hers. Not yours. When you read them out loud in class, I
could hear her voice. All that childhood magic and stuff.
The singsonginess. It all came back to me. It just isn't you.

I'm going to keep the Pegasus Journal hostage until you
agree to work with me on this project. I'll keep it safe, I
promise. But you have to write some of your own poetry
or I won't ever give it back. Tape your poem to the inside
door of your locker. That's how I'll know you are ready.

Love,

Niccolo

Thursday, April 14

Dear Lizard,

Last night I dreamed that Tess was standing next to my bed. She was a wolf. She was hungry and I had chocolate. I wanted to feed her but I didn't know the rules.

I asked you what we should do, but you kept running away every time I got close. I ran after you in the dark woods, screaming your name. *Lizzie. Lizzie.* But Tess was behind me, howling. It was high tide. I could smell the salt.

Do you remember the night she changed? Every time I hear a dog howling, I wonder if she's come back. One time I went to the window and looked out. It was a full moon. But Tess wasn't there.

Niccolo

BLOOD PROMISE

Lullaby, thou lupine beast
Sister wolf shall slay and feast
Plunge thy snout in supple flesh
Gorge and gouge, the blood is fresh.
Sister wolf, destroy the crèche
Lullaby, thou lupine beast.

Lullaby, thou Queen of Toads
Queen of Mice on muddy roads
Lady Lupus, howling trace—
Howl the moonlight from this place.
Virgin Mother, full of grace
Lullaby, thou Queen of Toads.

Lullaby, my sweet, good night
Break thy bread by pale moonlight!

BLOOD PROMISE

Sometimes, in October, just before the season gives way to the bitter wind that rises from the ocean and keeps us in wool sweaters until winter is over, we'll get one rare night when the air along the river is mild, a return to summer for just a moment, like a fever breath. Tonight is one of those nights. We beg Mamma to let us bring our sleeping bags and quilts down to the floating dock so we can sleep outdoors one last time, even though it is a school night. We promise we'll come in if it gets too cold. The moon is shining down on the water, low in the sky because it's still early. We're in sweatpants and wool sweaters. We've got Grandma Ruth's memory quilt wrapped around our shoulders. We call it the memory quilt because it's got little pieces of our family story in it: a patch from Mamma's prom dress, all powder blue and satiny, a soft-soft square from Tess's baby blanket, pink as the inside of a bunny's ear. There's a square from the first set of yellowy-yellow curtains that used to hang in our kitchen, the color of lemon drops.

Even though I love them all, the patch I know the best, the patch I always want to find with my fingers and rub against my cheek, the patch I know in my memory like the feeling of my mamma's hand, warm and smooth on my forehead, is the purple velvet patch from our Halloween costumes the year Tess and I each went as a unicorn. I remember. We had purple velvet leotards and Tess made wings out of paper. We pranced in step with our arms linked together and the smell of October all around: cinnamon, apples, and the hint of colder days coming soon. I rub the velvet patch against my cheek and lean against Tess's skinny shoulder. The stars are out. I can hear the clang of buoys and the foghorns. A seagull flies up from the surface with a huge blue crab in his claws. Our eyes follow him into the sky where the moon waits like a blind face. A warm wind comes up from the water. I pull the quilt tighter around our shoulders.

"Look," says Tess, pointing. "It's a full moon."

"A perfect moon," I say. The waves lap the wooden dock, and the creak of rusty hinges makes me sleepy. My eyes are heavy.

"I might turn into a wolf tonight," Tess tells me.

I smile and lean back against the wooden railing. The moon is yellow and heavy as a tablespoon of honey.

Tess gets down on her hands and knees and pads to the edge of the floating dock. "The last time there was a moon like this, I transformed. Nobody saw me, but I did. I crept down to the Amodeos' house and got caught in a trap and had to save myself by biting off my front paw."

She demonstrates this by sticking her wrist in her mouth and chomping down over and over again.

I giggle and lie down on my back. The stars wrinkle and gleam.

"Lizzie, I'm not kidding. Why don't you ever believe me?"

I yawn and find the purple patch with my fingers. "I believe you," I tell her. I'm grinning. I can't help it. I keep thinking about Tess chomping on her own wrists and the thought sends me into paroxysms of laughter, and the more I try to stop myself, the more I want to laugh until I'm fighting back tears and spluttering like a teakettle. But Tess isn't laughing. She's still down on all fours, circling and pacing and pawing the dock with her open palms. "This is serious, Lizzie," she whimpers.

"Serious," I say, trying not to smile.

"You have to keep watch over me tonight to make sure I don't go over to the Amodeos' and do something horrible." Her voice is low and growly and she hunches her shoulders like a wolf. "I might get into their house this time. They always leave their back door open. I might climb into Isabella's room. We'd wake up in the morning and there would be blood and hair all over my face. And then the police would come and I would go to jail. Lizzie, I'm going to need your help tonight."

The waves lap at the side of the dock.

Tess slams the dock with her open palms. "Promise me," she barks.

I sit up.

"If you want to see her alive in the morning, then promise me."

I put my hands on Tess's bony shoulders. "It's okay," I whisper to her, patting her head. "Come on. Let's try to go to sleep. It's getting late."

Tess grabs me by the wrists and her fingernails dig into me. She stares into my eyes. Then she raises her face to the moon and howls a long hollow note.

"Okay, okay," I tell her. "I'll watch over you."

"Promise me you won't tell Mamma."

"Okay, Tess. Okay. I promise."

"Blood promise," says Tess. And then, before the meaning of those words registers, Tess unclasps one of her silver unicorn earrings, and in one terrible movement she plunges the horn into the palm of her hand. One quick stab. One drop of blood rises to the surface of her skin like a tiny red blossom.

"Now you do it."

My heart has turned to stone. I have forgotten how to speak.

Her eyes shine. She reaches out and takes my hand. She strokes the tops of my fingers and my wrist. Slowly, she turns my hand palm up. I know what she is going to do before she does it, but I don't pull away. When the unicorn's horn jabs into the palm of my hand, it feels like a white-hot needle going deep. Then it's over. Tears well up in my eyes and fall. She watches this. She spits on the inside of my hand and rubs my hand across the dock.

"Now we're connected forever." Her voice is serene and sweet.

That night Tess rises from her pillow and pretends to be a wolf. I watch her like I promised I would. I watch her hunch her shoulders and pace the edge of the dock. I watch her pretend to run and pounce and snarl and rip and eat. Then I watch her bite at her own skinny white wrist. She chomps down again and again. I huddle in a corner of the dock with my knees pulled up to my chin. I find the purple patch of the memory quilt and hold it to my cheek in two clenched fists.

I sleep in fits and starts. Sometimes when I wake, she's curled beside me in the memory quilt, hands cupped like paws over her nose, growling faintly, twitching her legs like she's dreaming about chasing a rabbit. Other times she's standing on all fours at the edge of the floating dock sniffing the wind, bristling. But this time I wake because my hand is throbbing, and even though the air is chilly, I can feel the heat up my arm. I've soaked it in the salty river water and wrapped it tight with one of my kneesocks, but the unicorn wound still burns in the flesh of my palm. I peek under the dressing. Even in the moonlight I can tell it's red and angry. I want to go inside and let Mamma take care of me, but I promised Tess I wouldn't tell. I promised her I would stay up and watch over her tonight. I promised. I promised. I grasp my hand to my chest.

"Tess," I whisper.

She doesn't answer in English. She raises her chin to the moon and barks three short staccato notes.

"Tess, I want to go in. My hand hurts."

A foghorn sings out over the wind.

Tess lowers her head and hunches her shoulders. A low growl starts somewhere inside her belly. It sounds like the rumble before a clap of thunder. My teeth chatter. No matter how slowly I breathe, no matter how much I try to relax my body, my teeth clatter together like the keys of Mamma's electric typewriter, *clickety clickety clack*. I bring my wrapped hand against my cheek. My stomach is uneasy and now I am shivering uncontrollably, my entire body cold and hot at the same time.

"I want Mamma," I tell Tess. "I think I'm going to be sick."

Tess growls and shakes her head back and forth like a wolf tearing at flesh.

Now there are tears coming down my face. I kick my way out of the sleeping bag and creep backward toward the ramp. "Please. Please stop pretending. And let's go in."

"I'm not pretending," Tess snarls.

"Oh, stop."

"I really am a wolf."

"I can't play this anymore, Tess," I sob.

"Say you believe I'm a wolf."

"You're a wolf," I whisper, shivering.

"You don't believe it. Say it like you believe it."

I hug my hand to my chest. My fingers are starting to ache. "You're a wolf," I say, trying to make my voice sound certain. "You really are a wolf."

Tess grins and raises her head to the moon. Her red hair cascades down her back. I can hear her voice becoming more throaty and more threatening. The moon shines down on us. It casts shadows on the dock. I blink. Black fur begins spreading across her skin, darkening her wrists, her feet, her face. Within seconds her entire body is covered in black fur. Her face grows pointed and long, her mouth and nose extending so that now she has a snout and a wolf's teeth, shiny and white like knives. Her hands and feet grow into paws and her nails lengthen and curl. Tess opens her mouth and lets out a deep throaty howl.

"Stop it," I plead. "I want to go inside."

Tess stares into my face. Her eyes are yellow.

"I promise I won't tell. I just want to go inside to sleep. I want to take care of my hand. Please, Tess. I won't wake Mamma. I'll just go in and get a Band-Aid and come back. Please. Change back. I don't like you this way."

Tess barks once, bares her white teeth, and bounds across the wooden ramp and into the woods, her tail waving behind her like a flag.

I could leave her right now. I could head back up the hill to the house. I could wake Mamma and Daddy and climb into their arms and tell them everything. But I don't. It's past midnight. My sister has turned into a wolf. I promised I would watch over her. I can't break my promise. I stumble behind her, teeth clattering, clutching my wounded hand to my chest. She looks back and waits for me to get close and then she bounds away again, barking, breaking twigs beneath her paws. I screech her name into the night.

———

I chase her through the woods, stumbling over rocks and roots, over fallen leaves and broken rowboats. She is faster, running on all fours. She turns every ten feet or so, to make sure I'm still following her. If I drop too far behind she'll stop and dig in the dirt, or scratch herself with one hind leg, or chase her tail. Then, when I get close enough to touch her, she barks and bounds away again. My cheeks are tearstained and hot. I call her name into the night. *"Tess, Tess!"* I don't have enough breath. My call is swallowed up by the shadows and the trees. *"Tess, stop!"* She doesn't answer.

We cross through the woods to the Amodeos' rock garden. The moon is round and full. It casts a milky light on everything.

The world outside is full of shadows, blue from the pine trees overhead. Even with the moonlight, it's hard to spot Tess. Her fur is dark and she skulks around corners. I find her lying down beside the Virgin Mary statue with her muzzle flat against the earth. When she sees me, she digs her claws into the pine needles and whimpers.

"Come on home, Tess."

Tess growls.

"Isabella and Niccolo are asleep in there. You don't want to wake them up, do you?" I take a step closer to Tess and put my hand out to touch her.

The growl turns into a snarl. I lose my balance and stumble toward the Virgin Mary statue. Then the snarl grows into vicious barking. The enormous black wolf rises to its feet, head lowered, fur bristling. It throws its body between me and the statue. If I come any closer I know it will kill me. A light goes on in the Amodeos' house. I can hear voices in there, shouting. The older brothers.

The wolf lurches at the window, barking and howling madly.

Isabella pushes aside her curtain and peers out at us.

"Lizzie, is that you?"

There's a rustling inside the house, the low, muffled sound of voices. The creaking of stairs and footsteps. Then Isabella and Niccolo appear at the front door. Isabella has her arm around Niccolo's shoulders. The twins blink and shiver in the cold moonlight.

"Please be careful," I beg them. "I don't want anything to happen to you."

"You guys shouldn't be here," Isabella tells me. "Mamma and baby Joey are at Auntie Rosa's house and the boys are taking care of us. They think Tess is Captain Tom's old dog from down the street. They're ready to call the pound. What are you doing out so late?"

"My hand hurts," I tell her, choking back tears. "I think something bad is happening to me. I'm hot. My fingers feel funny."

"Why do you have it wrapped up in that old sock? Let me see what you did."

I unwrap the white kneesock and hold up my hand so Isabella can see.

She gasps. "Yuck, Lizzie, how did you do that?"

I don't know what to say.

"You look horrible. Tess, take Lizzie home right now."

The black wolf jumps toward Isabella, barking and snarling, baring its teeth, spit flying. It paws the pine needles and howls. Isabella laughs and pushes Tess back down on the pine needles.

"She wants to kill you," I say, sobbing.

"That's stupid. Go home and wake up your parents. Tell them you need to see the doctor."

The wolf crouches down. She stares into Isabella's eyes.

"She hates you because you're my best friend," I whimper.

"Well, she needs to get over it and take you home."

"I don't think she's going to do that."

"Tess," snaps Isabella, putting her hands on her hips in the moonlight. "Stop this bad game right now."

The wolf leaps at Isabella, white teeth flashing. It goes straight for her neck. Isabella falls backward into the garden wall. She grabs the wolf by the shoulders and tries to push it off her body, but the wolf is too strong for her. She kicks her feet into the wolf's stomach, but the wolf stands firm, its two front paws pushed into Isabella's chest. It sniffs at her face, nuzzling at her neck like it is looking for a place to take a bite.

Isabella screeches and slaps the wolf across the face but the wolf stays put.

"What the hell is going on out there?" It's the voice of one of the teenage brothers.

"It's that crazy old dog again!" calls Niccolo back toward the house. "I'm just gonna help it find its way home." Then he puts out his hand, palm down. "Here, girl," he whispers.

The wolf raises its head from Isabella for a moment.

Niccolo whistles and slaps his side. "C'mere, puppy. You hungry?"

It whines and licks its lips.

"Poor puppy," Niccolo says. His voice is quiet and desperate. My heart is beating. He shoves his hands into the pockets of his flannel pajamas. They are empty. "Wait here for me," he tells the wolf. "I can help you, but you have to let my sister go." The black wolf backs away from Isabella. It stalks to the Virgin Mary statue and puts its muzzle down at her feet. Niccolo charges inside the house. Isabella scrambles up from the ground. She brushes pine needles from her nightgown. She is breathing hard.

"I can't believe it," says Isabella. "He actually thinks she's turned into a dog."

"A wolf." I sniffle. "She's a wolf. And she almost killed you."

"You're all crazy. He's gone into the kitchen to get her a bone or something."

"Maybe that will help," I say, out of breath. "If it has a bone maybe it'll fall asleep and then I can carry it back up the hill. When the sun comes up it'll be Tess again."

"It's Tess *now*." Isabella frowns. "And there's no way you're going to carry anything with your hand like that. Oh Lizzie, I wish you would stop pretending and just go home. This is really serious. You need a grownup to look at your hand. You need a doctor."

There is the creak of the kitchen door opening and closing gently. Niccolo comes out and squats down on the porch steps. He pulls a Coconut Crunch bar from his pajama pocket. Slowly, slowly, he rips open the paper wrapper and holds the candy out for the wolf. "It's okay," he whispers. "I won't hurt you. You're a hungry girl, aren't you. This is good. Chocolate. Do wolves like chocolate? Delicious. See?" He smells it and licks his lips.

The wolf licks its lips too. Now I can see it must have been starving for months. Its bony pelvis juts up from its hind legs, and I can see the deep arc of the rib cage, the ridge of the spine and the shoulders.

Niccolo keeps holding out the chocolate bar. "You can have it. Come a little closer and take it from me. I won't hurt you."

The wolf approaches Niccolo with tentative footsteps.

"That's it."

The wolf comes even closer. Its legs are shaking.

"Easy now," says Niccolo. "You're almost there."

The wolf snaps the chocolate bar out of Niccolo's hand. Frenzied. It backs up toward the Virgin Mary statue and lies down in the pine needles. It worries at the chocolate bar, nosing it, licking it, growling faintly. Finally it begins to feed. Chomping down deliriously, whimpering. But it's over too soon. The chocolate bar is gone and the wolf is still starving. It snaps at the pine needles and licks the vestiges of chocolate from the fallen leaves. Niccolo is armed and ready. He has more Coconut Crunch bars in his pockets. He whips them out and unwraps them quick as a flash. "You're still hungry," Niccolo says. "You haven't eaten in so long, have you? I have more for you. I have lots more." And he lays them down at its feet and then backs away so that it won't be scared.

As the wolf eats, it begins to transform into a girl again. First the black fur pulls itself back into the skin like thousands of worms disappearing into their holes. Then the paws become hands, the claws become fingers. The snout and ears recede, leaving a girl's face in their place. The skin pinks. The eyes round, become more luminous, the features soften and bend until I can see Tess's face again, Tess's beautiful face, her long red hair falling over her shaking shoulders as she eats and eats, crouching in the pine needles, shoveling chocolate bars into her mouth, rocking as she chews and swallows, licking the chocolate from her palms and fingers.

There is one Coconut Crunch bar left. Tess carries it like an offering to the Virgin Mary statue, kneels down in the pine needles, unwraps it, and pushes the chocolate into the statue's white face. She smears the chocolate back and forth and back and forth across the tight red mouth. Then she stands and looks at me. Her face is streaked with dirt. There are pine needles in her hair.

"I want to go home," she whispers.

I hold out my hands and she comes to me. I wrap my arms around her shoulders and half carry her, half lead her, step by step, away from the Virgin Mary statue, away from the rock garden, and out onto the road where streetlamps cast a yellow glow.

She is my sister again.

We leave Isabella in the rock garden behind us.

"Lizzie, let me help you," Niccolo calls from the steps of his house.

I wave to him but don't say anything. Isabella turns on her

heel and heads toward him. They go inside and she closes the kitchen door silently. I stagger with Tess leaning into me all the way back down the cracked road and up the pine needle path to our front porch, where the hammock is an empty ghost that rocks in the wind. We climb up the wide pine steps, open the double doors, and shut them behind us, then up the winding staircase, and down the crooked hallway to Tess's room. She sits on the edge of her bed and holds out her arms so I can pull off her wool sweater and change her into the pretty white flannel nightgown Mamma keeps on a hook by her bed. I kneel down on the rug. I pull off her socks and sweatpants. I smooth the nightgown down to her ankles. Her freezing feet are tiny and beautiful. They soothe each other like doves, the toes of one foot sliding into the sole of the other. I lift her blanket and pat the clean sheet. She yawns, curling onto her side, nestling into her pillow, murmuring faintly. I tuck the blanket around her body. I kiss her cheek and turn on the golden night-light at the side of her bed.

"Lizzie?" It's Tess's voice, sweet, and muffled by the bed-clothes.

I don't answer. I have unwrapped the kneesock from my palm and have begun to touch the red edges of the hole. There are dark blue stripes, like lines of Magic Marker, running from the hole in my palm all the way up the inside of my arm. I touch my skin. My hand is on fire. I sway on my feet.

"Lizzie, bring me a glass of warm water."

I don't answer.

"Did you hear me, Lizzie? I'm thirsty. I need something to drink."

I take a step toward the bathroom. I sway on my feet.

"Lizzie?"

Everything goes black.

HOSPITAL WALLS

The hospital gift shop sells balloons—
yellow smiles with ribbons trailing down.
Get well soon. Get well soon. Cheerful words.

This one, I tell my mother, pointing upward.
I pull the wisp of ribbon. The yellow smile
bobs its head. At night I kneel beside my bed.
Oh Jesus, I whisper, *when she opens her eyes
let the balloon smile at her. Get well soon.
And she will. Because words don't lie.*

Time passes. The tide rises and falls.
The helium seeps into thin air. The balloon
droops. When she leaves the hospital to go home,
an orderly, some skinny candy striper,
with the face of an angel and the hands of a child,
takes the sheets off the bed. Throws the smile away.

When I see her again, she looks at me and smiles,
but her eyes are empty. And I wonder
why we swallow lies with ease, mouths open,
dutifully, like vitamins, or like pills to ease the pain.

Niccolo Amodeo

HOSPITAL WALLS

The room is white and only big enough for a bed and an armchair. A pale nurse comes in to take my temperature and to peek under the gauze strip that covers my hand. She jots something on a clipboard and smiles at me. Then she hurries out. It's quiet except for the steady rain outside the window, the *beep* of the machine on the wall, and the hum of fluorescent lights. There's a needle in my hand and a clear tube running up to a plastic bag that hangs from a metal pole by my bed. Clear liquid drips into the tube. *Drip drip drip.*

I know Mamma has been here because I see two empty Dunkin' Donuts coffee cups and a newspaper on the chair by the bed. Someone has brought yellow flowers and a yellow smiley face balloon. I reach over and pull the balloon down to my bed. I make it jiggle on its yellow ribbon like the head of a silly puppet. I make it talk to me in a voice like Mickey Mouse.

Hello, you little sicky pickle. Why are you lying in bed so sad and mopey?—I don't know, Mr. Smiley Face.

Mamma and Daddy come in. I know they're only pretending to be okay because their smiles look like they hurt and their eyes are full of shadows.

"The nurse told us you were awake," Daddy says. He kisses me on the head. Then he turns to Mamma. "She feels cooler. Good girl." He lifts up my chart, takes a look at my temperature. Then he puts the clipboard back on the table facedown and smiles at me again.

"How are you feeling, honey? Any better?" Mamma puts the back of her hand on my forehead. Her skin is smooth and cool. "You have such wonderful friends, Lizzie. If it wasn't for Niccolo we never would have known to look for you. He called us in a panic. He told us you and Tess were playing some game in the woods. Some kind of make-believe. I'm not angry. I won't punish you. The doctor wanted to keep you here because of the infection, but also because you are dehydrated and had a temperature. It's just for one more night. But I want to hear what happened from you, honey. I want to know how you got that horrible hole in your hand."

I turn my face and watch the rain come down.

"Lizzie," whispers my father, "did Tess do something to you?"

The rain makes trails of water across the dark glass.

Mamma reaches across the bed and turns my face to her.

"Lizzie, you have to tell us the truth." She pets me. Runs her hands through my hair.

Daddy puts his arm around her shoulders.

We stay like this for a moment, not saying anything. Just waiting.

I take a breath. "She stabbed my hand," I whisper.

Mamma sways on her feet. Daddy takes her to the chair by the bed and helps her sit down. "Go on, honey," Daddy says to me.

"She took off her unicorn earring and stabbed her hand first. Then she stabbed mine. And spit on it. And wiped it off on the duck. There was a lot of blood. She made me promise to watch over her. It was supposed to be magic. A magic promise."

"Magic promise," Daddy says through clenched teeth.

"Because she was turning into a wolf. It was a full moon. And she was worried about what she was going to do to Isabella. She hates Isabella. We played fairies without Tess once. And we took the rowboat. And sang rounds. And Isabella said we're best friends, but I don't want to be best friends if it means Tess will turn into a wolf and stay that way. She's my sister. I have to love her best." I am shivering again and tears come to my eyes.

"Oh, honey," says Mamma. "Shhh. Shhh. It's okay." She gets up from her chair and comes back to my bed. She climbs in beside me. I lean against her, burying my head into the side of her neck where it fits like a pillow. She smells like coffee and cigarettes and hospital antiseptic, and she holds me and holds me.

"I chased her but I couldn't make her come home. She was so fast. And my hand was hurting. I promised I wouldn't tell you any of this. I promised I would watch over her and never tell anybody. I didn't want to break my promise. Mamma, I told Tess I wouldn't break my promise."

"You didn't," Mamma whispers into my hair. "It wasn't a real promise. It was make-believe."

"She tried to bite Isabella, but Niccolo came out with chocolate bars and Tess was so hungry she ate a ton of them. I helped her walk back up the hill. I put on her nightgown. She asked me for a glass of water. I was so tired. And my hand hurt. And then I fell down. That's all I remember."

"When we found you both, you were lying unconscious by her bed and Tess was fast asleep, snoring like a princess." Daddy smiles bitterly. "With her white nightgown, and her feather pillows, and her pink quilt all tucked in."

"I tucked her in," I say. "I remember I tucked her in before I fell."

"She tucked her in," my father says, his eyes smoldering. "Do you hear that? Are you listening?"

"Stop it, Marty. Don't make it worse."

"How could it be worse? Really. How exactly could it be worse?"

My eyes fill with tears. The question hangs unanswered in the tiny white room.

Dead Crabs and
Sea Glass

The best time to look for sea glass is after a thunderstorm. The waves shift the layers of mud and new things that used to lie just under the surface are revealed at low tide. Sometimes I find shards of blue willow tea sets from the old days. Other times I find thick black glass from sailors' wine flasks or raggedy brown shards of marmalade jars. I am released on Saturday, and on Sunday all I want to do is search for treasures. I take a spaghetti pot down to the river and train my eyes to find patterns and colors in the mud. Sometimes what looks like a clamshell is really the side of a soup bowl. Turn over what looks like a brown rock, and you might find the handle of a water jug. That first day home this is what I want to do most. Just walk back and forth along the windy river looking for things to keep.

"Do you want to play Crab Carcass Bingo?" Tess asks me.

She is sitting, bundled up, on the floating dock with her hood around her ears and her collection of dry bodies. "I found a fabulous crusher rock. You could use it. Come on, Lizzie. I missed you. Play."

"No," I tell Tess. "I'm doing something else right now."

"I can't play it by myself," she whines.

"Well, do something else then."

It is cold. I hunch my shoulders down into my sweatshirt.

Tess turns back to the crabs. She finds a big one and moves its claws back and forth. "I'm coming to get you," she croaks.

"Oh, please." I continue looking for treasures. I find two emerald-green bottle necks poking up out of the mud like turtles. I wipe them on my sweatshirt and drop them in the pot.

"Can I look for treasures with you?"

"No," I say. "I want to do it by myself."

My back is to her so I can't see her face, but I know from the way she is breathing that I've hurt her feelings. I don't care. Hurt feelings are nothing compared to the unicorn horn going into the palm of my hand. They are nothing compared to passing out and hitting my head on a cold floor while my sister sleeps like a princess. They are nothing like two nights in the hospital with an IV in my arm.

"Lizzie," says Tess. "There is something strange going on."

I don't say anything.

"While you were gone, Mamma started watching me. Staring at me. When I'm home, she won't let me out of her sight for a minute. She walks me to my classroom in the morning and she's right there at the end of the day. She sticks to me like glue. Look. She's watching me now."

I look up the path. It's true. Mamma is sitting a little ways up on the wooden bench overlooking the water. She has a quilt around her shoulders, and she sits with her manuscript and a mug of tea. She keeps looking down at the dock to make sure we're okay. I wave to her and smile. She waves and then goes back to editing her manuscript.

"I can't do any magic with her around," Tess complains. "Do you know how hard that is? I feel like I'm going to pop, Lizzie. You have to help me get away from her. You have to hide me."

"No, Tess, I'm not going to do that," I say. I turn over a shard of white pottery. There are fragile green willow leaves printed all along the edge. I wipe it on my shirt and place it in my spaghetti pot. That's a good one.

"Merlin says a wizard needs to keep practicing magic or else he'll lose his spells."

"I'm sorry to hear that, Tess," I say. I know how cold my voice sounds. But somehow, the words feel good.

"Lizzie, did you tell Mamma about what happened that night?"

I turn and look at her but I don't say anything. She sits on the floating dock surrounded by dead crabs. She is skinny. Way too skinny. And her red hair needs to be cut. No one has hair down to her waist anymore. No one but plastic princess Barbie dolls. I suddenly fight an urge to take her red hair in one fist and pull so hard that her head snaps back.

"Did you break the blood promise and tell her about my powers?"

I take a breath. "Yes, I told her everything."

She looks up at our mamma and scowls. "Did she believe you?"

"What do you mean?"

Tess is standing now, her fists clenched around two dead crabs. "I mean, did she believe you when you told her that I turned into a wolf and ran through the forest looking for meat? Did she believe you when you told her how I ran on all fours with my tail waving behind me like a flag? Did she believe you when you told her how I howled at the moon? How my wolf fur glistened under the night sky?"

"Of course she didn't believe me, Tess."

"Why *of course?*"

I take a step toward her. "Because it wasn't real," I say, my voice deadly calm. "Because it was all make-believe and you know it."

"You take that back."

"I won't."

Tess is shaking, every fiber of her body tensed and furious.

I can see her teeth clench, the muscles of her jaw working like crosscut saws.

"No. You will. You believe in magic. Say that you believe in magic, Lizzie."

"I don't believe in magic. I have never believed in magic."

Tess makes a sound. It isn't exactly a scream and it isn't exactly a cry. It is something else. The sound of humiliation and betrayal. It sounds like a mirror shattering. "You're lying! You've seen the magic work. Transformation. Flying. Ghost voices. All of Merlin's lessons. You've been with me. You know it's true."

"I was playing. I was just playing, Tess."

Tess shrieks.

Mamma rises from her bench. She hurries down the ramp and stands behind Tess. "Calm down," she says.

"Yes, Tess. Calm down."

Tess shrieks again. She takes the crabs, one in each hand, and crushes them into her hair. There is a crunching sound, and then Tess is rubbing the shells into her scalp, the legs breaking, the brittle red backs. "Stop it," says Mamma. "You are out of control. Stop it right now, Tess."

Tess falls to her knees on the dock and weeps. She flings handfuls of dead crabs out across the river. She throws one after another, screeching and pitching. The tide is starting to come in. The dead crabs float away, a parade of dry bodies. Tess is making so much noise I can't even hear the seagulls.

Mamma sits down cross-legged behind Tess and holds her while she flails and weeps.

"Lizzie!" Mamma shouts to me over the ruckus. "I'm going to try to help your sister calm down. Do you hear me? I want you to go away from her for a while."

I nod.

"This isn't your fault, baby, okay?"

I nod.

Tess struggles in Mamma's arms.

"Go over to Isabella's house. I'll come get you when things are better. Go on, honey. Everything is going to be okay. Mamma is going to take care of everything."

SACRED HEART

I have never been to a real Catholic church before, but when I tell Isabella what happened with Tess, she says we really have no choice. We'll go to St. Anthony's, where no one knows her, and if we pray really hard, Christ will forgive us for breaking the rules. We'll take Tess's bike and my bike and ride downtown in the waning light, all the way past the bed-and-breakfasts, across the drawbridge, down the sleepy boulevard with fish markets and pizza places on one side and the quiet harbor on the other, and up the hill where the tiny white steeple of St. Anthony's chapel looks out over the ocean like a heron. We enter silently. Isabella takes my hand. It's dark except for the dim light from the candlelit cross at the front of the chapel with the form of Jesus Christ, his hands stretched to either side, his head bent, his feet nailed together.

"I shouldn't be here," I whisper to Isabella.

"Anyone can come and pray," she says. But her hand, clutching mine, is cold.

"There aren't any other Jews here."

"You're my friend. And you've been sick. And now Tess is in trouble. I know it seems wrong, and I know people might get mad if they knew, but this is the only thing I can think of that might help."

Isabella leads me to a pew near the front of the chapel where she kneels on a red velvet step and folds her palms in front of her face. I sit on the smooth wooden seat beside her. There aren't many people in the tiny, dark chapel, just older women, the wives of fishermen, who must be praying that the traps will come up full of lobsters and that the men will come home with their boats and bodies in one piece. They hold their rosary beads between beefy fingers and look up at Jesus on the cross. Their prayers rise and fall like boats.

"In the name of the Father and the Son and the Holy Spirit," Isabella whispers.

I close my eyes. "*Baruch atah Adonai, Eloheinu melech ha'olam.*"

Isabella taps my leg. "Pray to Jesus," she whispers, her voice shaking. "We came all the way down here so you can do it right. Come on, Lizzie. Cross yourself and tell Him what's happening. It's the only way you can get the help you need."

I try to cross myself like I did in Isabella's bedroom, but it feels wrong to do something so Catholic in a real live chapel with the statue of Jesus Christ watching us. So after I touch

my forehead, I put my hand over my heart like when we have to pledge allegiance in school. On Yom Kippur Mamma knocks at her heart while she prays, so I curl my hand into a fist and bow back and forth the way I've seen her and Daddy do. It's hard to bow sitting down in the pew, so I lower myself to the red velvet step and kneel beside Isabella. I close my eyes and knock on my heart, and I try to summon up a picture of Tess in my mind. I imagine Tess standing on the floating dock at low tide with her fists curled around two dead crabs. I imagine her slamming the two dead crabs into her hair, shrieking like Medusa, her skinny face contorted, all open mouth and eyes, the hollows of her skull showing beneath her skin. I wish I could cry. I knock on my heart and bow like Mamma and Daddy and I picture my sister's horrible face in my mind, but nothing happens except a cold feeling.

"This isn't working," I whisper to Isabella.

"Please," she says. "Just give it a chance."

After a while, there is a swell of music from the organ up front. It fills the chapel and makes me dizzy. Two men come up front. Lizzie explains that one is the priest who leads the service and the other is a deacon who assists him. They both cross themselves and begin to sing. The women in the pews sing back to them. I let their songs wash over me and watch the candlelight flicker. We sit and stand and sit again. Finally, the women begin to file out of their pews and make a line. Isabella takes my hand and, heads bent, we join them. The priest whispers to each of the women and puts something on their tongues. The deacon lets them sip from his golden cup. They swallow and cross themselves, then they return to their pew. The organ swells and rises and swirls in the little chapel. It smells like cinnamon and oranges and I find myself swaying on my feet.

I've never been this close to a real live Jesus on the cross. He is skinny like Tess, with his ribs sticking out, and he wears a white cloth around his waist so no one will look at his private parts under there. I know he must be in pain, because there are nails going through the palms of his hands. It doesn't hurt anymore, but you can still see the place where Tess stabbed me with the unicorn horn. Jesus Christ holds up his chest and tries to breathe. But it's not going to work. It's just a matter of time when his arms will get tired and his rib cage will get tired and he will let himself drop into nothingness. Just like that. Crack. And then poof. He's gone.

Isabella stands in front of the priest but does not look at him. Her hands are shaking. She opens her mouth and he places something on her tongue that looks the same as the little round matzo cracker Grandma Ruth used to serve with her chicken soup. He tells Isabella it is the body of Christ. She says, "Amen." The deacon hands her the golden cup. She holds it in two hands like a baby who has just learned to drink and she takes a sip. Her eyes are closed. She looks so helpless.

When she swallows, she has a smile on her face as if she is tasting something delicious. Then it hits me. She thinks she is eating Jesus Christ's body and drinking Jesus Christ's blood. And she is smiling. She wipes her mouth with the back of her sleeve before moving on down the line.

Now it is my turn. I take a step forward. There is no turning back. The priest is standing in front of me. My stomach turns. I am Jewish. What am I doing here? *Baruch atah Adonai,* I whisper in my mind, but I don't know the right prayer to say. *Oh my God, oh my God. What am I doing here?* I want to tell him this is all a mistake. I want to tell him I wandered into the wrong building, that I thought this was the local synagogue, that I am sorry but I wanted to pray for my sister and I got lost and found my way here.

The priest says, "The body of Christ."

I whisper, "Amen." And then I have no choice but to open my mouth like a baby bird and let the priest place the body of Christ on my Jewish tongue. When the deacon puts the golden cup in my hands, I am afraid my fingerprints will sizzle and my skin will be singed, but the cup is cool to the touch and the wine is sweet. I swallow. Jesus Christ slides down my throat. He slides into my belly. I have bones and skin and hair and blood and veins and sinews and brains inside me. I have fingernails and intestines and lungs and bowels inside me. I have thumbs and knuckles and kneecaps and blood vessels and body hair inside me. I sway on my feet. The church lurches beneath me.

Instead of going back to the pew, I make a run for it. I charge past Isabella, past the fishermen's wives and out the huge wooden doors where the world is full of shadows and there's the smell of salt water and pizza and the cold harbor below, and I hear waves and the sound of boats and church bells and my own jagged sobbing as I heave the body and blood of Christ out of my belly. I sink to my knees and shriek all my sorrow onto the pavement.

ORANGE JUICE AND HAPPY PILLS

D r. Orca tells Mamma that the pills will help Tess stop
believing in magic. Mamma cries a little, but says thank
you very much and goes to the pharmacy to fill the prescrip-
tion. Every morning and every night, Mamma makes Tess take
a blue-and-white capsule with orange juice. She places the pill
on Tess's tongue and Tess swallows it down obediently.

Tess says they can't force her to stop believing in magic,
but Mamma thinks this is just the disease talking, and once
Tess starts feeling better, the magic will go away and never
come back. *Poof.* Like a dragon winking out of existence. Tess
has to see a shrink doctor twice a week after school. That's
what Daddy calls Dr. Eugenia Orca, whose office is in the
center of town, high up on the top floor. Dr. Eugenia Orca of
the wonderful name, and the wonderful Spanish accent, and
the wonderful black, black hair all tied up in braids around

her head. She is the one who will help Tess turn away from Merlin and live in the real world instead, just like the rest of us.

Daddy says they call people like Dr. Orca headshrinkers because their job is to shrink perfectly good heads like Tess's. Headshrinkers also shrink your wallet. He says when Dr. Orca is done with Tess there will be no more money left to pay the bills, and Mamma says, *Stop saying things like that. You'll scare them.*

I'm not scared of Dr. Orca. She lets me sit in the waiting area while Tess goes in to talk. Sometimes Mamma goes in with Tess and they both tell the doctor things about our family. Other times Tess goes in by herself. Dr. Orca has a radio in her waiting room that she always keeps tuned to the classical station, and she always has at least four issues of *The New Yorker*, which Mamma and I both like to read. Mamma reads the essays and short stories. I like the cartoons. I sit with a November issue and scan through the pages for a cartoon I can understand. In this issue, most of the cartoons don't make sense to me. Here are two old people sitting on a couch together trying to turn each other on with remote controls. The caption says *Modern Love*. I smile and show the cartoon to Mamma even though I have no idea what it means.

She pets my hair and I swing my legs. They always keep the heat pumped high in Dr. Orca's building, and the waiting room is filled with the soft hiss of warm air coming up from the heating vents. The leather armchairs are set away from the closed office door so we can't hear anything going on when Tess is inside being shrunk. Every once in a while, Mamma or I turn toward the closed door because we think we hear a cry, or a sob, or a giggle, or something else that might tell the secret of what Tess is saying about us in there. But mostly we just wait, page through *The New Yorker* and think our own thoughts about who that girl is going to be when all this shrinking is over.

At four o'clock Dr. Orca opens the office door.

Tess is standing there, grinning. This is the fourth appointment, and her head still does not look the least bit smaller. Maybe Daddy was wrong.

"Tess, why don't you go ahead and sit down next to your sister over there. I'd like to discuss one or two things with your mother before you go."

"Okeydokey, Dr. Orkey," Tess says in a cartoon voice, still grinning madly. She spins over to an armchair and flops down. Then she turns to me and crosses her eyes. I glare at her.

"Lillian? Do you have a moment or two?"

My mamma places her copy of *The New Yorker* back down on the coffee table.

"Of course," she says. "I have all the time in the world. Girls, will you be okay out here without me?"

"Oh yes, Momsy, we'll be just fine." Tess swings her legs up so she's sitting Indian-style in the chair. She leans toward me and folds her hands in her lap like she is going to tell me a story.

Mamma glances at me.

"Go ahead, Mamma," I say. "It's okay."

"It will only be a minute," says Dr. Orca.

Mamma gives a weak smile and follows the doctor into the office. The door closes behind them. At first we don't say anything to each other. I pick up *The New Yorker* and pretend to read. There's a symphony playing on the radio. There are too many violins moving their bows too quickly so it sounds like a swarm of angry bees. I put the magazine down. Tess is still leaning forward and grinning at me.

"So what did you do in there today?" I ask Tess.

Tess looks sideways at me. "Well, mostly I talked and cried."

"What did you talk and cry about?"

"I make things up. Today I told her that I was going to set our house on fire. I like to make her worry. She has such a cute little nose when she's worried. It gets all wrinkled up. Like a pug." Tess imitates Dr. Orca, pushing her nose up so I am looking inside her nostrils.

"You mean you lie?"

Tess huffs in disgust. "You make it sound so criminal. You think I'm going to tell some shrinky-dink doctor the truth? This lady doesn't even believe in magic. And she wants me to stop believing in Merlin. I'm not ever going to do that, Lizzie.

It would be like dying. So today I told her that I was going to set fire to Mamma's curtains."

"Tess," I say, "I think you're supposed to tell her about real things."

Tess glares at me.

"Dr. Orca can't help you get better if you don't tell her the truth."

Tess rolls her eyes. "You've gotten so boring, Lizzie," she says. "Like a cow chewing her cud. Grass and hay. Munch munch munch. Too bad. I always liked you."

"That's not fair."

"Life's not fair, sister."

Tess uncrosses her legs and gets up from the chair. She paces back and forth in front of the closed door. When she hears the doorknob turn, she dashes for the armchair again. When Mamma and Dr. Orca come out she sits there like a princess with her legs crossed all prim and proper.

Mamma's face is ashen.

Dr. Orca looks at Tess. "Are you going to try to remember the things we talked about today, Tess? And put them into effect before we meet again on Friday?"

"Will do, doc," says Tess. She pantomimes lighting a match and setting the curtain on fire. She waggles her fingers like flames.

Dr. Orca gives Mamma a look. Then she looks over at me. Her eyes soften. "Lizzie, your mother and I talked about whether you might like to come in and meet with me on Fridays as well. Would you like that?"

I don't say anything. My stomach is tight and I think I am going to throw up.

"I'll talk to her about it," Mamma says. "I'll give you a call tomorrow once we've all had the chance to think. Thank you so much for everything, Dr. Orca."

Dr. Orca shakes Mamma's hand. "Keep on giving her the medicine. And remember, we're upping the dosage. Two pills every morning and two every evening, with orange juice. And call me if there are any concerns, okay? There shouldn't be any side effects, but if there are, I want to know."

"More pills?" squeals Tess. "Oh goody!"

Mamma frowns. She puts a hand on Tess's shoulder.

"And I do hope you'll come talk to me, Lizzie. What Tess is going through can't be easy for you. Think about it. Okay?"

"Okay," I whisper, looking at the rug beneath my feet. "I'll think about it."

On the way home, Tess falls asleep in the back of the car, and I sit in the front with Mamma. We drive in silence down the boulevard, past the harbor.

"I don't want to talk to that doctor, Mamma," I tell her.

"Okay, honey. You don't have to."

"And Mamma?"

"Yes, Lizzie," Mamma says. She is looking straight ahead, driving the car, her fists clenched tight on the wheel.

"Tess told me that she isn't telling Dr. Orca the truth. She's just going in there and lying. She makes things up and pretends to cry."

Mamma puts her hand through my hair, but keeps looking at the road. "I know, honey," Mamma says. "Dr. Orca told me. And she also said that sometimes with a child like Tess, the things she makes up can be significant. Even the lies are worth listening to. I think Dr. Orca has a pretty good handle on things."

"I hope so," I say. "I really want Tess to get better."

"Me too," says Mamma.

———

That night, before we get into our pajamas, Mamma gives Tess two blue-and-white capsules with orange juice.

"These will make you feel better," Mamma says.

"I don't want to feel better," whispers Tess, her eyes wide and pleading. "I like being like this. Mamma. Please. I want to stay the way I am."

"That's just the sickness talking," Mamma says gently. "You keep taking the pills. Soon none of this will matter to you. You'll forget all about it. I promise."

"I don't want to forget."

"Of course you do. We all want you to be well, Tess. Can't you see that?"

Tess nods. Her eyes are filled with tears.

"Good girl. Now open your mouth. I have the pills and the orange juice. You like orange juice. Here you go."

Tess lets Mamma put the two capsules on her tongue. She holds the orange juice in her hands like a little baby learning to drink from a cup. Then she closes her eyes and swallows.

Mamma throws her arms around Tess.

"I love you so much, sweetheart. You know that, don't you?"

Tess nods wordlessly.

We go upstairs to brush our teeth. I take out my green toothbrush and squeeze a line of toothpaste across the top.

Tess does not touch her toothbrush. She has tears in her eyes. She raises the toilet seat with trembling hands, spits the capsules into the water, and flushes. The two blue-and-white pills swirl and swirl in the water and then disappear.

I open my mouth to call to Mamma but Tess reaches out and touches me on the cheek. Her hand is warm. I close my eyes for a moment, rest my cheek on her palm. Then she hugs me. She hugs me so hard, I can feel her whole body press against me. She is so small. Sometimes I forget how small she is.

"Lizzie," Tess says. "Please don't tell. I'll never do that again. I'm going to be good and get better. I promise. I promise."

———

She does not get better. At night Mamma and Daddy argue about what to do. I can hear them below the floorboards, talking about how it isn't working. Dr. Orca tells Mamma there's a hospital nearby that takes children Tess's age. A famous place, where kids can stay until they are out of trouble. There are doctors and nurses who can watch her every moment. *Think about it, Lillian. Please. She'll be safe there. And they'll help her get better. I know you're trying hard to make things work at home, but this might be too big for you to handle on your own. Will you think about it?* And she hands us a pamphlet with pictures of children painting at easels and walking in gardens and holding hands with their parents, their faces filled with grateful smiles.

Mamma promises to think about it. She brings the pamphlet home. Puts it up on the refrigerator door with a magnet.

"We can't afford it," says Daddy. "Besides, I can't believe you want strangers taking care of our daughter. We can manage this at home."

Every morning and every night, Mamma gives Tess two pills with orange juice. Tess stands perfectly still with her eyes closed and her mouth open. Mamma places the pills on her waiting tongue and gives her the juice. Tess always nods to show it is finished, and Mamma smiles and kisses her on the head. Tess never spits them out in the toilet again. I know because I spend every moment I can with her. When Isabella wants me to come over to play, I lie and say I have too much homework to do. I close the front door and listen to her footsteps down the porch steps. At school, I make excuses to sit by myself. I don't want a best friend. I want Tess back.

Then one night Daddy goes up to change her bed.

"Lillian," Daddy screams down to the kitchen. "Come up here."

Mamma comes up with Tess. They are holding hands.

Daddy picks up the mattress to show her. Pills.

"Oh Tess," says Mamma.

Tess falls to her knees. She is undone.

Mamma and Daddy don't speak. Slowly, systematically, they ransack her bedroom. They open her dresser. They slide their fingers into rolled-up socks. They shake the bindings of books. They turn her pillowcases inside out. They find pills tucked away here and there, hidden like insect eggs.

"Oh my poor sweet baby," says Mamma.

"From now on, I am in charge of this," my father says.

"Marty," says Mamma. "Please."

"I'm in charge," he shouts, as though saying the words louder a second time might make them come true.

Daddy pulls Tess off the floor by one arm, wrenching her backward. He stands behind her, pinning her arms to her sides. He grabs two blue-and-white pills from their nest under the mattress and slams them into Tess's mouth before she can struggle away. Daddy holds one big hand over her face. "Swallow them," he says.

Tess is weeping. She thrashes her head back and forth against his chest.

"Marty," Mamma pleads.

Daddy holds on. "Swallow the goddamned pills, Tess."

"Let her go, Marty."

"Swallow the goddamned pills!"

He whirls Tess around and smacks her across the face.

Mamma screeches and begins to weep.

I put my hands over my ears and back away toward the door.

I don't know how long we all stay there like that. Daddy with his hands on Tess's face. Mamma weeping in the corner. Me cringing by the door with my hands over my ears. Maybe it is only a few seconds and maybe it is an hour. I can't tell. Because time seems to stop, and everything in the world swirls around this moment like a vacuum cleaner, taking up all the air and drawing it into its bottomless lungs. But at a certain point, either moments or hours later, Tess swallows and motions to her throat with her hands. Daddy wrenches her mouth open. He runs one finger across her gums, under her tongue, and behind her teeth to check. When he is positive she has really swallowed the pills, he kisses her face, takes her into his arms, and cries in her hair like a baby.

From then on, Tess takes her pills. Wordlessly, with eyes as empty as Dixie cups. She swallows them. Two every morning and two every night before bed. She opens her mouth and lets Daddy place the blue-and-white pills on her tongue. She holds the cup of orange juice between her two shaking hands and she swallows and swallows. Soon the magic will go away, Dr. Orca tells us. It will dry up, little by little until there is none left, not even a drop. She will forget how to turn invisible. She will forget the language of the seagulls.

On December 2, Mamma takes the hospital pamphlet down from the refrigerator. She replaces it with Tess's new drawing. It is a square house with a triangle roof and two big curtained windows in the front. There is a yellow sun in the corner and a family all with smiling faces. They are holding hands in front of a garden filled with flowers. There are no jagged lines and no shadows. There is no poem. She does not sign her name at the bottom.

DEEP RIVER

She comes to me just before dawn, curling behind me in bed, her skinny arms around my waist, her toes scraping the heels of my feet. She whispers magic spells into my hair, words I could understand if I opened my eyes, but the sounds hiss into my blankets like wind from an open window and I stay submerged in dreaming.

I dream we are horses cantering together, our arms linked, our knees stepping high like Merlin taught us. I dream we have manes and tails that trail behind us, and moonbeam wings uncurling from our shoulder blades like smoke. Now we are lifting over the river at high tide and into the air together. She holds my hand while we fly. We look down at the river from above, the floating docks, the fishermen's boats, the empty summer houses with their decks and windows.

Tess tosses her head and whinnies. It is a sound like laughter and church bells.

I dream that we are wrong about her. Dr. Orca and Mamma and Daddy and Isabella and me. We are wrong. Tess does have magic. She has always had magic. And I was wrong to stop believing. She comes to me on the dock with her hands cupped over something special, something she is hiding, like a piece of sea glass or a hermit crab. Something alive. I come close. She opens her hands and there on her palm is a white glow that crackles and leaps from her skin and grows to surround us both.

We are laughing. Twirling in the white light together, our arms raised up over our heads, our white nightgowns swooshing around us, our hair all loose and pretty. We twirl and laugh and Tess sings *Row, row, row your boat* as loud as she can. She sings for an audience of seagulls and herons, for pipers and plovers and egrets. *Row, row, row your boat Gently down the stream. Merrily, merrily, merrily, merrily, Life is but a dream.* They love her. They flap their applause, swirling around her like fairies. I sit on the floating dock and clap and clap until my hands break like shards of glass, like wind chimes. Oh, Dr. Orca, you are wrong about her. She is something new. Something that has never been real before on this earth. She is a Pegasus. She is a selkie. She is the queen of toads. You do not have my permission to destroy her.

I take the blue-and-white capsules and I fling them across

the river. They patter onto the surface of the water like bread crumbs raining down. And all at once the river is full of fish, fish of every size and color, fish with luminous ribbons streaming from their tails, fish with golden fins and eyes the color of opals. The world is filled with the sound of their teeming, the slap of their tails against the water. They rise to the surface in swirling droves and devour every capsule in a frenzy of mouths and scales. We watch them in our night-gowns, our arms around each other, the moon shining down. We watch them until every blue-and-white capsule is gone, and the fish bow their heads and sink one by one back down into the river.

"Do you believe me now?" she whispers to me in my dream.

I don't know when the dream ends and what is real comes back into my dark bedroom. At some point, she closes her cupped hands. The white glow disappears, and we are holding each other in bed, our eyes open. I know I have been crying. My face is still wet and Tess reaches over and wipes my cheek with the back of one thin finger.

"I have to go," Tess tells me. The dream has ended, but the magic is still there. I am looking at my sister.

"Where are you going?" I whisper.

"A real selkie can swim back into the ocean and be a seal forever. That's what the legend says. A real selkie can leave her human skin on the shore like a bathrobe. She can slip back into her seal self and swim away. I don't want to take the pills anymore, Lizzie."

"You have to take the pills to get better," I whisper, still half-asleep.

"I don't want to get better. I want to keep the magic. I'll visit you," she says. "I'll be in the ocean. You can call me whenever you want and I'll come. Lizzie, I know it's all been make-believe to you, but just for tonight, just for this one last time, please tell me you know the magic is real. I'll never ask you to believe in it ever again."

I rub my eyes and look at her. She is staring at me intently, as if by staring she could will me to believe. She reaches out and strokes my hair. I love her. I love her so much. She puts her forehead against my forehead and breathes on me.

"Please, Lizzie. Please."

I pull away and look at her. She is so small.

"The magic is real," I say, with tears in my eyes. I kneel on my bed and really look at her face for the first time in weeks. Her eyes are shining. Her hair is long and tangled and she is so thin she looks like she could blow away. I hold her hands and bring them up to my face.

"Jump in with me," Tess says. She kisses the tears on my cheeks. "I want you to be the last human I see before I swim away."

"Stay here," I sob.

"No, Lizzie," Tess says. "This is the way it has to be. But you will always be my magical sister."

In our flannel nightgowns, goose down comforters, and woolen socks we tiptoe out of my bedroom, down the stairs, and into the dark kitchen. Here is the woodstove, the stained-glass lamp, the old high-backed chairs, all cast in darkness. Here is the tide chart, the spaghetti pot, and the sideboard. She takes my hand. We go out on the porch. There is a wind blowing. The tops of the pine trees sway and bend. We stand at the porch railing and look down across the road at the river. Even from here you can see it's high tide. The trees have lost their leaves. When the cold wind blows, the bare branches reach into the sky like dancers.

"We need to hurry," whispers Tess. "It will be morning soon. And selkies can only transform when the moon is out."

"We should go back to bed," I tell her.

Tess reaches for my hand and pulls me down the porch steps, down the pine needle path, and across the cracked road. I follow her onto the dock, down the ramp, and across to the floating dock. There hasn't been a tide this high in a long time. The hinges on the ramp squeal every time the waves carry the float to rise and fall. The moon is out and we can see the reflection of the pine trees on the water. We stand on the edge holding hands and shivering. I look down into the cold, black water. It is a long way to the bottom.

"I'll never let you go, Lizzie," Tess whispers. "No matter what happens to me, I'll never ever let you go." She takes my hand and turns it over. She kisses the scar on my palm. "The selkie king is waiting for me. I have to go. Now I am going to count to three and we will jump together. But you will come up human and I will come up a seal, and I'll wave a flipper when I swim away. I love you, Lizard."

"I love you too," I whisper.

We let our comforters fall onto the dock.

All of a sudden, the wind claws across our skin.

Tess begins to sing a spell in her magical language. It is the language of selkies and winged horses.

Achem moon poon yung jung bo
Nardo pardo don lem syo
Caballero moon poon cho
Pinto minto song sing so.

"Are you ready to leap, my magical sister?" Her voice is gentle.

"It's too cold, Tess."

"Don't be scared," says Tess. "Say *nardo pardo*."

"*Nardo pardo*," I whisper, my teeth chattering.

"Say it louder. Say it like you believe in it."

"*Nardo pardo!*" I say.

Then she shouts the numbers into the night: "One, two, three!"

We leap off the float in unison. For a moment before we fall, we are suspended in midair, our legs hovering over the river, our arms outstretched, our mouths open, our eyes open, turning toward each other for just a fraction of a moment, the very tips of our fingers touching.

Then my body plunges into the water.

Tess lets go of my hand.

There is the sudden shock of winter on my skin. I let my body sink down to the bottom of the river. There is no light from the moon under the water. I begin counting like I always do. *One. Two. Three.* I make my body heavy. I slow my feet and arms, moving just enough to stay under. Tess can hold her breath for longer than anyone I know. *Four. Five. Six.* It is only freezing at first. After the first few seconds, the water becomes more like fire. It grips my scalp and the back of my neck. My arms and legs are burning. *Seven. Eight. Nine.* And then my heart starts beating in my ears and my throat constricts and it feels like my lungs are about to collapse. *Ten.* I kick my feet and allow my body to rise back up to the surface. I break through the water. I gasp for air. I pull myself back onto the dock and wait for Tess to come up. My nightgown is plastered to my legs. The moon shines down. I have never been this cold in my life. I wrap the two goose down comforters around my head and my body and I wait for Tess, shivering violently.

Seventeen. Eighteen. Nineteen. I hug myself and look up at the stars.

Any moment now.

Thirty-five. Thirty-six. Thirty-seven.

She can hold her breath for longer than anyone I know.

The dock rises and falls on the waves.

Fifty-eight. Fifty-nine. Sixty.

There is a gust of wind. The tops of the pine trees bend.

Seventy.

Somewhere from far off, there is the clang of a buoy.

A dog barks.

Seventy-nine. Eighty.

I lose track of the numbers.

Finally Tess's human skin comes up from the bottom of the river. It floats facedown, arms trailing behind, white nightgown lifting above the waist. I reach into the freezing water and pull on the hand so the body can float closer to the dock.

It is as icy and stiff as a fish.

The body turns silently onto its side.

The empty face gazes at me, the lips pulled back in a smile.

WITHOUT TESS

When you bury an old woman, no one makes too big a deal about what goes into the coffin besides the body. I remember how it was when we buried Great-aunt Beverly. Mamma and Daddy helped Great-uncle Mendy pick out the yellow chiffon dress, the one with the ruffles down the front, and they wanted her to wear the opal ring Great-uncle Mendy gave her on their fiftieth wedding anniversary. Of course there was conversation about open casket or closed, about what kind of makeup, and about the wig. I remember they brought a color close-up to the undertaker so he could try to make her look swarthy. Mamma said she just wouldn't look like herself unless he made her dark. All those summers on Brighton Beach. But in the coffin Great-aunt Beverly didn't look swarthy. She just looked dead.

No one discussed whether Great-aunt Beverly should be

buried with the things she loved most in the world. They didn't, for instance, bury her with the wooden ladle she used to stir her chicken soup, or the sheet music to *Hello, Dolly!* which she could play most of the way through without looking at her left hand. They also didn't bury her with her favorite fancy hand towels, the pink tasseled ones with the little embroidered primroses along the edge. No one deliberated over whether they should bury her with the pink knitted toilet-seat doilies, or the macramé owls, or the sad-eyed puppy dog rugs. Even though in life Great-aunt Beverly collected fancy-restaurant sugar packets, which she arranged in chronological order above the door of her kitchen, and even though she took them down before every Passover to dust them off and reminisce with Great-uncle Mendy about their good fortune to partake in fine kosher meals at quality establishments such as Kutsher's or Brickman's, and even though she had just collected her last sugar packet on her fiftieth wedding anniversary—just fifteen days before she died—no one even thought to discuss arranging her sugar packets around the satin pillow of her casket.

But it's different when a child dies. When a child dies, she leaves behind a bedroom filled with stuffed animals and toy horses and books that have been read a thousand times with the pages all dog-eared and torn. She leaves behind hairbrushes with strands of long, snarled hair still tangled in the bristles. She leaves behind a Pegasus Journal with pictures of unicorns tossing their heads, and girls in princess dresses, and wizards with gnarled staves in their hands, and fairies with gossamer wings that spread from one side of the page to the next. She leaves behind pictures of toads with little girls in their mouths. Sketches of children drowning. Sketches of faces with dark, bleeding eyes. Sketches of sisters howling at the moon. When a child dies, there's all this horrible, beautiful stuff left behind and no one knows what to do with it.

The objects themselves mock us. Everything in the child's room tells us she is coming back. The white nightgown is washed and hung neatly on a hook. The undershirts and panties and the pure white tube socks are still in the laundry basket. The pillowcase smells like her hair. If you lie down on the bed with your face on the pillow and breathe in, it is the living scent of her skin that comes to you. The smell of her asleep and breathing deeply. And if you wander around in bare feet so that your toes sink into the rug, if you wander around and touch things with the very tips of your fingers, let them glide like feathers across her quilt, her walls, her desk, her dresser, if you spin very fast in circles the way she always used to do, and let the death room swirl around you like a cocoon wrapping you in white silk threads, you could imagine that at any moment she is going to explode through the door, laughing with her mouth wide open at the perfection of this final joke.

But it is not a joke. Because downstairs there is a rabbi sitting with your parents at the kitchen table, and they are talking about what he should say—about how he should focus on who she was before things got bad. It is not a joke because they have photographs of her face spread across the kitchen table and they are looking at them with dry eyes because there are no tears left. It is not a joke because here you are, in her empty bedroom, trying to follow the rabbi's instructions to find something "meaningful" to place in her casket. *I often ask the sibling to do this, as a special kind of goodbye.* And so you stand there in her room, letting the objects unwind around you, the horses and Pegasus Journal and clothes and . . . and . . . and . . . and then, and then, and then it's me, and I am standing in her room and I am Lizzie without Tess. I am Lizzie without Tess. I am Lizzie without Tess. And I am real. And she is gone.

I lie facedown on her bed with my head on her pillow. I breathe and breathe.

PEGASUS JOURNAL

They bury her in the pink ruffled shirt she wore for school concerts. The one with the mother-of-pearl buttons that go down the front, and the sleeves that flare at the wrists. They put on her unicorn earrings and a necklace with a Star of David that Grandma Ruth brought back from Israel. The casket is filled with things that Mamma and Daddy and I picked out from her room. Stuffed animals. A toy horse. Some old photographs and, of course, the Pegasus Journal. The undertaker has arranged these things around her body and folded her hands so she would look more casual. Her job is to make the body look like Tess. She has put special makeup on her so her cheeks look less gray and her lips less blue, but to me it is all wrong.

In their attempt to put color in her skin, they have made her look waxy and too dark, almost orange. There is something about the way the eyelids are closed that makes me look twice. Are they sewn shut? Are those threads underneath the skin? No eyes close so tightly. When you are asleep there is always a little space, the promise that the lids could flutter open at any moment and the moist, expressive eyes could move and see. But these eyelids are locked. This painted doll is not Tess. Tess would never brush her hair so carefully or arrange it around her face like this in perfectly styled tendrils. She would never cross her arms like this. She would never lie so still in a room filled with people who know her. As I approach her casket, I half expect to see her squirming. Fidgeting. Anything but this. In the end, it is the absence of movement that makes her look most unlike herself. Even if her face was the right color, even if her hair was uncombed, her eyes resting lightly, I would know that this wax statue was not my sister.

No one sees me do it. Or if they do, they don't say anything. I bend over to kiss her. I touch her hand. And in one swift movement, I grab the Pegasus Journal out of her casket and hide it in the inside pocket of my coat. I can feel it in there, a weight against my leg, all the way back to our seats and, later, at the graveyard, I can feel it poke against my body every time I take a step. When I walk with Mamma and Daddy to the grave it is there. It is there when Great-uncle Mendy and Uncle Irving and Uncle Morris and Uncle Ben carry Tess's casket on their shoulders and place it on the bier. It is there when they lower her into the ground, the slow muffled creak of the box going down. It is there when Mamma's cousin Max leads us in the Mourner's Kaddish. Mamma and Daddy stand on either side of me. The words of the prayer swirl around us and around the open grave like doves.

Yit'gadal v'yit kadash sh'mei raba
B'alma di v'ra khirutei v'yam likh malkhutei
B'chayeikhon ub'yomeikhon
Uv'chayei d'khol beit yisrael
Ba'agala uvis'man kariv v'imru amein.

I can feel the Pegasus Journal push my leg when the rabbi calls me up because it is my turn to put my hand on the shovel that Daddy has left for me in the pile of brown dirt. Now it is my turn and the rabbi helps me put the spade into the pile and pour the earth and stones from the shovel down the hole, six feet down, through the darkness, and onto the wood of the casket where Tess's face would be if she were looking straight up.

I have never heard the sound of earth hitting a casket before. It is a hollow sound, a thump that rises back out of the hole and shakes you, because the person in there can't hear it and because your hand is on the shovel that is burying her. Mamma, Daddy, and I move off to the side, our arms around each other. People from our family take their turns. Aunts and uncles. Cousins. Then people from the neighborhood.

Here is Mrs. Caruso, her head all covered in a black veil. Here is Miss Stephanie. They each take a turn, plunging the shovel into the pile and filling in the hole. The sound changes as the casket is covered. The thump becomes more muffled. Less resonant. But there is so much more to do. Even after Niccolo, who is at the very end of the line, puts his small, bare hand into the pile of earth and drops the dirt down into the hole with his fingers, the casket is still only barely covered, and the rectangular hole still yawns. After we finish hugging one another, after we finish nodding and saying we are okay, after the last car leaves the graveyard, following the limousines back to our house, the graveyard men, whose job it is to make sure things get done, will stay behind and finish on their own. They will work together to do it fast without tears or prayers. One shovelful at a time, they will bury the casket in dirt and fill the hole and then they will walk away and leave my sister in the earth.

———

The ride back from the cemetery is a blur. I sit between Mamma and Daddy in the back of the limousine. Then everyone is at our house for shiva. They eat coffee cake and drink hot tea and they talk to Mamma and Daddy in low voices downstairs. They come in and out of the rooms, clucking their tongues and comforting one another. Mamma's once-a-month writing group is here. I spot the poet with her high-heeled black boots and the picture-book writer with her blue spiderweb veins and her red potato feet powdered and pushed into loafers. Mrs. Caruso is here with a pot of tomato soup. The Amodeos are here, Isabella and Niccolo both wearing their Sunday best. Isabella is wearing her silver cross. I reach out and touch it, but I don't know what to say. Isabella looks down at her feet. Miss Stephanie brings a casserole still hot in its pan, and a white funeral lily. She sits with Mamma in the kitchen and tells her how sorry she is. Cousin Max stands on the porch by himself and looks out at the water. The kitchen is packed with food and flowers and people who have come to pay their respects. But even with the house completely full of guests it feels strange and empty. It is a new kind of silence that I can hear even when everyone is talking at once.

I tell Mamma and Daddy that I need to go up to my room to change out of my fancy clothes. I take Tess's Pegasus Journal out of my coat pocket. I run my fingers over the spiral binding, letting the tip of my finger play each curled wire like a harp string, up and down. I put the notebook up to my cheek. It's still warm from its place inside my coat. It smells like Tess. Like salt water and pine needles and sweat. I don't open it. Someday I will. Someday after years have passed I'll sit with it and I'll look at the pages and I'll remember. But not now. I still ache too much. And I'm afraid that the pictures and the words will be so powerful and so frightening that they will pull me under the water with her and I will drown. For now, my own memories and my own sadness will be enough. I find an old box in my closet. I wrap the Pegasus Journal up in Tess's white nightgown that I've taken from her room and lower it into the box. I close the lid and push it back into the corner where I will find it when I am ready.

RANSOM

Every time I open my locker, the absence of Tess's journal expands and deepens and swirls like a vortex so it seems that the inside of that narrow space has suddenly become a terrible vacuum. When I reach for my math book or my history binder, all I can think about is the absence of the journal. When I swing my backpack from its hook, or when I reach down to find my running shoes for gym, I try to turn my face away, but it isn't possible to avoid an object that is not there. Every time I try not to notice, I notice it more.

For some reason, the thing that bothers me most is the old wool sweater I've always used to hide the journal, still rolled into a ball on the top shelf. Each time I get ready to close my locker door, I adjust the sweater by force of habit, making sure the journal is hidden from view. Now, even if my eyes are focused on the hallway, my hand knows that there is nothing there. All I can feel is wool and the cold slide of metal beneath. At the end of the day, when I shoulder my backpack, the lack of the journal makes me feel I have forgotten something essential, so all the way home, I find myself looking back over my shoulder. I can't sleep at night. The backpack hangs open on my chair, heavy with the wrong things.

"I can't stand it," I tell Kaplan at our next session. "I need it back."

"Yes," Kaplan agrees.

"I don't know what to do. What should I do?"

Kaplan looks at me. He is not smiling. "I don't have an answer."

"I can't believe this, Kaplan. I'm asking you a direct question. Just this once. Tell me. Tell me what I should do to get back my sister's journal. I can't live without it, Kaplan."

Kaplan looks at me from across the desk. "I'm sorry," he says. "This has to come from you, Lizzie."

"I hate you," I tell him. "I really hate you sometimes."

"You hate yourself," Kaplan corrects me. "And you don't need me to tell you how to fix this. You can do it by yourself."

———

I stay up all night. I write a poem of my own. It isn't a work of art, but it's mine. In the morning, I tape the poem to the inside of my locker. In the afternoon, it is gone, and I know that

Niccolo has it and that at the very end of the day we will meet face-to-face, and we will talk.

The last-period bell rings. Kids erupt into movement, glorying in the freedom of a spring afternoon stretching out in front of them. They reach into their back pockets and flip car keys into their palms. They shoulder backpacks and book bags. Isabella walks by me. For the first time in more than five years, I meet her eyes and smile. She smiles back. I lean against the lockers and play with my choke chain while I wait for Niccolo. More groups walk by, tight as hives. More car keys. More book bags. More laughter. Soon there is no one left but the janitors and no sound but that of teachers locking up their rooms, calling out to each other in tired voices, laughing their goodbyes. Finally, just when I am ready to give up, Niccolo appears. He has a skateboard under his arm and a package wrapped in newspaper.

"Took you long enough," I scold him.

Niccolo punches me in the arm. "Just wanted to see if you were really committed to this. But hey! You stayed and waited for me. I'm truly touched. Ready to get to work?"

I shrug my shoulders.

"I know a perfect place on the pier if you don't mind a walk."

"I don't mind," I say.

"Let's go then. Want me to take your books?"

"You think I can't handle them?"

He laughs and links his arm through mine. We

walk together, out of the school and down the road to the boulevard. I have to take two steps to keep up with every one of his long, easy strides. I never would have guessed that he would grow tall like this. He was always such a little boy, smaller than Isabella even. Now there is something about him that reminds me of a wild horse. His legs and arms are long, and his thick, black hair falls down to his shoulders, falls over his eyes so he has to sweep it back with one hand. He has lost the baby boyishness that I remember and now his face is full of angles. I watch him stride ahead. I like to see him move. How could I not have noticed this before?

Niccolo turns and slams his skateboard down on the concrete. "You are too slow, Lizard Cohen," he shouts. "If you keep stopping like this we will never get there." He motions to his skateboard with a flourish. "Hop on my magic carpet, baby. I'll take you for the ride of your life."

"I don't like skateboards," I say, smiling in spite of myself.

"Well, then you've never been on one." He laughs. "And besides, this is not a skateboard. It's a magic carpet. And it's waiting for you, Princess Lizard." Niccolo skates back to me, cackling maniacally, his eyes shining. He takes my poetry folder out of my arms and zips it up in my backpack. Then he swings my backpack onto his shoulder. He leads me by one hand onto the front of his skateboard. Then he gets on behind me. I can feel him push off with one foot and then stand pressed behind me, his hands around my waist. My back is warm from the heat of his body. There is the sound of our wheels rolling across pebbles, a grinding, swooping noise like rain. We swoop down the sidewalk, past the pizza stores and bed-and-breakfasts, past the bait-and-tackle shop, past the hardware store and the grocery store, and onto the pier where the tourists walk back and forth, taking pictures of the boats, looking out at the waves. Niccolo zips through the crowd. People jump out of the way, scattering like a flock of pigeons. Before I know it, I'm laughing out loud, and Niccolo's behind me, laughing his crazy laugh, pushing us onward to the side of the pier where there are benches and picnic tables and people sitting quietly looking at the water. The magic carpet stops. He takes my hand and twirls me toward a bench near the hot dog vendor. I drop down, my heart still beating fast, my face flushed.

Before I can say no, Niccolo hops up to the vendor and orders us two chili dogs with cheese and two Coca-Colas. He brings them to the bench with a smile as wide as a Cheshire cat's. "I knew Lizard Cohen would like skateboarding," Niccolo breathes. "Closest thing to flying there is. As I recall, the Cohen girls always liked to fly." I nod. I try to hold back the image of me and Tess linking arms, turning into horses, and flying into the heavens with outstretched wings. Niccolo sits down next to me and puts his arm out on the back of the bench. I lean my head against it, and he moves closer.

For a few minutes we don't say anything. We just sit on our bench with our dogs and drinks and watch the people pass by: young mothers pushing strollers, elderly couples with their arms around each other. We have never sat this close together before. When I was ten years old, Niccolo was Isabella's quiet brother. He played harmonica and watched us with dark eyes. Now he is grown. His arm is around me and even though I am the same person I was, even though the ten-year-old Lizzie is still in there somewhere, aching, shivering, hiding like a turtle, there is something about his touch now that makes me want to break into blossom.

"I'm glad we're sitting here," says Niccolo.

"Me too," I whisper.

"Are you ready to take it back? I have it here for you if you want it."

"I'm ready."

He opens up his backpack and takes out Tess's Pegasus Journal. He holds it for a moment before placing it in my hands. "I used to watch her scribbling away in this," he tells me. "I'll never forget it, this skinny girl with long red hair, bent over this little journal with her pencil scratching back and forth and such a serious look on her face. I never did get a good look at what she drew in there. I wanted to but there was never the right opportunity. I remember one time we looked up the hill from the road and she was there sitting on your porch just sketching away. I wanted to go see what she was drawing, but Isabella wouldn't let me go. Said that Tess might hurt me if I went too close."

"It was Isabella she wanted to hurt. I think she always kind of liked you."

"I liked her too," Niccolo says. And then he wipes his eyes. "I'm sorry," he says. "I'm not used to talking about this. After the funeral was over, after the first few weeks when the whole neighborhood took turns bringing you food so your mother wouldn't have to cook, when all of that neighborhood stuff was over, we all just stopped talking about it. You never came over anymore. Isabella made other friends. Your mom and dad started keeping to themselves more. It was easy to just kind of block it out and try to move on."

"I never moved on," I tell him.

"I know, Lizard," Niccolo says. He pulls me to him. "Neither did I."

"You still think about her?"

"Every day," Niccolo tells me, his tears flowing freely now. "Every time I jump off our dock, I imagine the two of you. Every time the moon is full and I hear a dog howling, I remember that night she turned into a wolf. There was not a single day in all these years that I didn't look up at your house and wonder if you were okay. I wanted to come up and talk to you so bad, but I just couldn't get myself to do it. So I kept my mouth closed and I followed your lead, and I ignored you just like you wanted me to. Until Lozano's class, I heard you reading these poems, these childlike, magical poems, and I knew I couldn't ignore you anymore. I needed this, Lizard. I needed this chance to say goodbye." Niccolo kisses the face of the Pegasus Journal and hands it over to me.

I take Tess's Pegasus Journal from him.

"I'm going to tell you something," I say. "Something I haven't told anyone. Is that okay with you?"

Niccolo nods. "You can tell me anything," he says.

TELLING THE TRUTH

Tess's death wasn't just a swimming accident," I say.

"You mean it was suicide," he whispers. "I figured that, Lizard. We all did—"

"No," I interrupt. "I mean, there's more to it than that. Tess was seeing a psychiatrist and taking medicine that was supposed to help her know the difference between what was real and what wasn't. The pills and the therapy were supposed to help her stop believing in magic. She was going to be normal. No wizards. No flying horses. But she didn't want to change. She said if she had to stop believing in all those things, she would rather leave the world. Swim away. Never come back. That night she told me she was going to turn into a selkie. She wanted me to come to the dock to watch the magic. I thought it could happen. I thought maybe just this once, maybe the magic could work." I reach out blindly and find him. "I was so stupid. I let her jump into the water. I let her drown. I didn't even try to save her."

"You were only ten years old," he says. "You didn't think she would go through with it."

"I was an idiot."

"You were scared. And nothing you could have done would have changed anything. Do you hear me, Lizzie? I'm telling you the truth. Tess's death was not your fault."

I am weeping now, my head buried in his jacket. I never wept at her funeral. I never wept afterward. This is the first time I've wept in more than five years. Slowly, the numb feeling seeps away and is replaced by something raw and sad and overwhelming and real. The images come flooding back. And I weep and rock as I tell Niccolo Amodeo the whole story. How jealous she was of me and Isabella. How she stabbed my hand with the unicorn earring. How I went to the hospital and returned angry. How I tried to pray but nothing worked. How the doctor prescribed pills. How Mamma wanted her to go to the hospital but Daddy didn't. How we leaped together off the dock. The shock of cold water on my skin. How I waited for her to turn into a selkie. Counting every second until it was too late. How her body floated up. How Mamma and Daddy came running down to find us seconds later, me on the dock hugging my knees, shivering uncontrollably, Tess floating next to me, grinning at the dawn, with hermit crabs tangled in her hair.

"They never asked me to explain. Daddy jumped in and pulled Tess to shore. Mamma put her arms around me. Daddy carried Tess and Mamma helped me walk back up to the house, still shivering, teeth chattering like castanets. After the coroner examined the body, we told neighbors and the relatives and the school that she had drowned in a swimming accident. When we told the story to each other, we talked about how cold it was that night, how strong the tide can get. How she was too small and too skinny to make it to shore. How she was always playing games in the water, always pretending. But this time it had gone too far. No one asked why my hair was wet too. No one asked why my nightgown was soaked. They threw our nightgowns in the dryer. Put the comforters up in the attic. We buried her and tried to move on. But no one moved on. All we had was this huge silence in the house, following us from room to room like a ghost. All the untold stories yawning out the space between us. Until all I had left of what really happened was the Pegasus Journal."

"And the poems," he says.

"And the poems."

We look at each other. Our eyes are red from crying and our faces are smudged from all the pencil and charcoal in the Pegasus Journal. Niccolo has a long, gray smudge down the side of his face from wiping away tears. I can't help myself. I break out laughing. And then Niccolo is laughing. All at once, we are laughing and crying at the same time. We wipe away each other's tears. And then we kiss away each other's tears, and then before we know it, we are pressed against each other, our lips opening, hungry and warm. He holds me and rocks me and we kiss and cry and laugh and kiss some more. We touch each other's hair. We trace the lines of each other's faces. And finally, when the kissing slows down, we bury our faces in each other's shoulders and we hold each other and breathe, our hearts beating, our blood moving because we are alive. We are alive. We are alive. And for the first time in five long years, I am free.

RESURRECTION

The window of his office is wide open, and every time the wind comes up from the harbor, I can smell summer coming, a gradual shift in the air, like a little girl breathing fever-breath next to your cheek. Kaplan sits in his chair and I sit in mine. I look across the desk at him, the same kind eyes, the same sandals crossed at the ankle, and he waits for me to speak, just as he always does. But for some reason, it already feels different from other Wednesdays because I know that today will be our last session. We've been preparing for this. Talking about it for weeks. He has told me it doesn't have to be good-bye. I can stop by and see him next year whenever I want. I know that's true. I also know I'll pass him in the halls when he's knocking wayward students on the head. Calling them little twerps. Telling them to stop scaring their English teachers. But it won't be the same.

"You did good work, Lizzie Cohen," Kaplan tells me.

"Thanks," I say. I can't find the right words for what I want to say to him, so I sit in silence. I am aware that I am blushing, and I wonder, briefly, why, after all these Wednesdays, I am suddenly feeling shy now, on our very last day together. I begin to laugh, realizing how ridiculous it all is.

"Why are you laughing?" Kaplan asks me.

"Because I am trying to think of a way to say thank you, and I realize that there just isn't a way to say it, so instead, I'm sitting here staring at you and not saying anything."

Kaplan smiles. "That's a perfect thank-you," he says gently. "I don't need any other."

"I feel good," I tell him, smiling. "I feel lighter."

"You've been carrying a sad story inside you for a long time. Now you don't have to be alone with it. It makes sense that you feel lighter. And I hope that as time goes on, that feeling will continue to grow."

"It's not over," I tell him, but when I listen to my words I realize that really I am telling myself. "I'm sad she won't grow up with me. And I still miss her. I will always, always miss her."

"Of course," Kaplan says. "She was your sister and you loved her. But you don't have to feel responsible for what happened. Now you know that you are just a regular human being who was not powerful enough to stop a tragedy from happening."

"I couldn't save her."

"No," Kaplan says sadly. "You couldn't save her."

I sigh and lean back into the chair. "I think I can live with that."

"It won't be easy," Kaplan tells me. "But you are on the right track now."

Above my head, the wooden horse turns on its strings. The glass of its red eyes reflects the sun. I reach up and touch one curled hoof. My finger comes away covered in dust. "I'm going to miss this guy," I say.

Kaplan pulls himself up from his chair behind the desk. He unhooks the wooden horse from the ceiling, touches its head for a moment, and then zips it into my backpack. "Take him with you," says Kaplan.

The bell rings. Our time is over. He walks with me to the office door.

"Can I give you a hug?" I ask him, grinning at my own nervousness.

"Of course," says Kaplan, opening his arms.

I give him an awkward hug. "Okay," I say. "Thanks again."

Kaplan smiles. "Anytime," he says.

I swing my heavy backpack onto my shoulder. I walk out the door.

———

When I get home, I hang the wooden horse in Tess's bedroom window, overlooking the river. He will like it here, watching the tides come in and out. Watching the sailboats and fishing boats, the mudflats and the birds. And when I feel lonely for Tess, I can come and sit on her bed. I can touch his hoof and watch him spin on his strings, his red eyes catching the sunlight.

A car door slams. I can hear the sound of heavy boots clomping across the porch.

"Marty?" Mamma calls from the kitchen. "Is that you?"

"Yup," Daddy says. "Home early."

Then there is the uncomfortable triangle of our silence again as we turn back into our own spaces. Daddy on the porch, Mamma in the kitchen, me up in Tess's room, all connected in our inability to speak to one another. Like three mimes, all in our own invisible boxes. Then, moments later, I hear the screen door slam. Beneath the floorboards, the sound of my father walking into the kitchen to join my mother in silence.

I find my backpack, sagging, almost empty, by Tess's bed. I reach my hand in and pull out the poem.

"Mamma," I yell down the stairs. "Daddy. I have something I want to show you." I rush down to the kitchen, clutching the paper with one hand. They are waiting for me, surprised and smiling, unused to the sound of my voice in the house. "It's something I wrote," I say breathlessly. "A poem. About Tess."

"Oh, Lizzie," Mamma says.

I take their hands and pull them to the table. We sit together, Mamma on one side of me, Daddy on the other. I smooth the paper out on the table, wiping the wrinkles away with the side of my hand. I rub away the chili-dog stain, clear my throat, and begin to read. I have never read my own writing out loud before, and it sounds strange to hear my words, tentative at first, then more assured and confident, tumbling into the kitchen. But I don't stop. I read the whole thing through. Even when Mamma breaks down and begins to weep, smiling, her eyes so full of so many different things, I can't do anything besides touch her hand. Even when Daddy gets up from his place at the table and stands behind me so that he can put his hands around my shoulders and around Mamma's shoulders at the same time. I can feel the warmth of their bodies as I read, and the warmth feels good. From somewhere, down by the river, we can hear a seagull singing.

WITHOUT TESS

Here are some things
I want to remember:
a toad blowing bubbles,
the taste of high tide
and pine needles,
crisp and fragile as salt—
the sound the river makes
when waves lick the dock,
a white, watery hush.
I remember the stain
of blueberries
on my fingertips,
the taste of September
stinging blue and sweet
on my tongue. I remember
wings, moonbeam thin,
fragile as gossamer,

how it felt to lift my arms
and fly.

She taught me
how to believe in magic,
how to swallow spells
without water, letting them
slide down my throat like
egg whites.
She showed me
how to run my tongue
over a lie, keep it safe
in the corner of my cheek
so I could taste it every time.
But now years have passed.
My jaw aches;
my tongue is parched.
I long to unclench,
part my chapped lips,
let the truth
finally slide through my teeth
white and clear as rain.

ACKNOWLEDGMENTS

Special thanks to my parents, Stan and Jackie Fleischman, who have taught me the importance of memory. To my sister, Marilyn Brown, who knows magic is real, especially if it comes in the form of an orange bracelet. Thanks to my dear husband, Stephen, and my sons, Joshua Andreas and Benjamin Kasiel, who hugged me when the story made me weep. To Alan Pollack, who appears in these pages in veiled disguise. Thanks to my wonderful friend and agent, Sally Ryder Brady, whose infectious enthusiasm and unwavering belief always pushes me forward. And finally, I give my deepest gratitude to my editor, Margaret Ferguson, who knows how to find order in chaos and who has the very rare ability to hold a thousand details in her heart at once. Her eyes helped me to see the shape of this story, the delicate pattern of past and present, of loss and redemption.

GOFISH

QUESTIONS FOR THE AUTHOR

MARCELLA PIXLEY

©Jill Goldman Photography

What did you want to be when you grew up?
I always wanted to be a writer. For as long as I can remember, I loved telling stories. When I was in preschool and kindergarten, I used to tell stories into a tape recorder. Then once I learned how to write, I began keeping a journal, which I carried with me everywhere I went. I would write down things I saw, things I heard, snatches of conversations, lists of ideas, details from dreams and nightmares. Throughout my child-hood, I filled almost thirty journals. I still have most of them in my writing room, spiral bound, leather bound, yellowed, and dog-eared. They are my most treasured possessions. Some of them have even made their way into my stories. In fact, my favorite journal, a spiral-bound notebook named Clyde, is the inspira-tion for Miriam's journal in *Freak*.

What's your favorite childhood memory?
In the summers, my family used to live right near a tidal river in Gloucester, Massachusetts. I loved low tide, because that is when all the creeping creatures came out, the fiddler crabs that scurried sideways, the hermit crabs, picking their way across the mudflats in their borrowed shells, and if we were lucky, we

might even catch a glimpse of the gigantic horseshoe crabs that only emerged on special occasions. If you sat still on the dock, you could watch the wading birds come in to fish for crabs. My favorite was the great blue heron who walked down the river-bed with long, yellow legs, and always seemed to be looking out into the distance.

As a young person, who did you look up to most?

The person I looked up to the most was my Grandpa Sidney. He used to tell me stories about when he was a little boy growing up in Divin, which was a shtetl in Poland. He had nothing but a red cow and a tiny, one-room hut with a grass roof. He told me about how he used to be hungry, and how he would cry to his mother for milk. He also told me about how his father, Jakob, saved up for a long time so the whole family could come to America and start a new life here. My grandfather never had the chance to go to high school or college, but he had natural intelligence. Everything that came out of his mouth was a poem. He had a beautiful lyricism in his voice. And I loved to listen to him. His stories made me want to tell my own. It is the greatest gift any human being has ever given to me. Now that he is gone, it is his voice that I miss most of all.

What was your favorite thing about school?

I loved being part of *Horizons*, the afterschool literary magazine led by my three favorite junior high school teachers. We met once a week after school, and brought our own poetry and short stories to read out loud to each other. We were a quirky bunch of kids. None of us conformed to the rigid structures of popularity that seemed to exist in the 80s. Some of us didn't feather our hair or wear blue eyeliner. Others didn't own the right brand of blue jeans. Some of us watched *Star Trek* religiously. Others memorized words from the dictionary. It was hard to fit in during the school day. But when we were together in *Horizons*, we knew we would be with other kids who would accept our differences. For that hour, we didn't care about being popular. What we cared about was writing. And for that hour, once a week, we were real writers working together.

What were your hobbies as a kid? What are your hobbies now?

Here are some things I loved as a kid: playing the cello, eating lobster (especially with butter and potato chips), pretending to be a unicorn, trying to move objects with my mind, watching *Star Trek*, singing, writing (of course), and playing make-believe games.

Here are some things I love now: writing, reading, walking in the woods behind my house, trying to train my crazy Golden-doodle puppy not to jump all over us, going on insane cross-country car trips with my family from Massachusetts to New Orleans, Minnesota, Wyoming, or Utah, singing at the piano with my kids and my husband, eating sushi, and collecting sea glass and pottery.

What was your first job?

My first real job was as a live animal volunteer at the Boston Museum of Science. Our job was to clean the animals' cages, mix their feed, and handle them so that they became used to human contact. We had screech owls and ferrets, wood ducks and possums. Most of them were animals human beings had tried to keep as pets that ended up being too unruly. My favorite was Hank, the porcupine. You had to wear padded gloves to handle him, and it took bravery because when he was mad, he would bristle. There was also a kinkajou named Honey Bear who had huge, round eyes and a prehensile tail that could wrap around your arm. They called him Honey Bear because he was honey colored, but also because he secreted this strange, sticky substance called "mung" from a gland near his shoulders. It was kind of gross, but I loved having all of this bizarre animal knowledge.

What is on your nightstand now?
A copy of *Autobiography of a Face* by Lucy Grealy
A Passover Haggadah
A gold locket that my Grandpa Sidney gave to my Grandma Dorothy
A cup half filled with tepid chamomile tea
A tattered copy of the Bach Suites for cello

How did you celebrate publishing your first book?
I bought a row of peach trees to plant in the back of the house. Now every August, when the peaches are ripe enough to pick, I think about *Freak* and how glad I am that I never gave up on my dream. It makes the taste of these peaches even sweeter. I think of them as victory peaches. And at the end of the summer, I make peach preserves so that I can taste the sweetness of that dream all year long.

Where do you write your books?
I have a wonderful writing room. My house was built in 1730, and the ceiling in my writing room has raw boards and beams. One beam still has bark on it. Can you imagine how old that bark must be? My writing room is filled with things I like to look at. Things that help me get into the right frame of mind for writing. There is an antique rolltop desk with an embroidered purse and a cameo that my mother gave me one year for my birthday. There is a collection of glass bottles from the woods behind my house. There is an old wooden box filled with letters. There are photographs of my family and a bookshelf filled with journals

and my favorite books. I feel at ease when I am in my writing room. It is one of my favorite places on earth.

What were you like in middle school?

I was a nonconformist. It used to bother me when people tried to follow the crowd: wearing the same clothes, the same makeup, listening to the same music, talking about the same television shows. So I went out of my way to be unique. I listened to classical music. I played Dungeons and Dragons. I kept on playing make-believe games long after most girls had stopped, and in seventh grade, I still had stuffed animals that I played with regularly. One time, I came to school with my hair done up in three ponytails, two on either side, and one on top like a unicorn's horn. The more other students rolled their eyes or made fun of me, the more I separated myself from them, telling myself that they were beneath me because they were not bold enough to be strange. It wasn't until college that I learned how to accept other people, as well as myself. It is okay to fit in. It is also okay to express differences if you want. One important thing I did not understand then is that one person can do both of those things. You can be part of the crowd sometimes and you can stand out sometimes. You can also protect yourself and save your strangeness for the people who you can trust to love and respect you. Human beings are vastly more complicated and more beautiful than I imagined back then.

Did you keep a journal? Do you keep one now?

I have kept journals my entire life, and I continue to keep them. There is something very satisfying about filling a page with writing and then another and then another. I have always loved the experience of looking back at old journals and seeing how I have remained myself even as the years went by. Even though my "voice" changes as I age, and even though I have become an adult with a husband and children of my own, I see myself shining in those journals from when I was a child. I didn't know it then, but writing in a journal has given me a way to talk to myself. The twelve-year-old Marcella can speak to the forty-three-year-old Marcella and tell her she is still a child deep down inside. The forty-three-year-old Marcella can speak to the twelve-year-old Marcella and tell her that everything is going to be okay.

What challenges do you face in the writing process, and how do you overcome them?

I think the most challenging part of the writing process is making the time to write. Life can get so full, and there are so many things that pull me away from my desk. There is the dog wanting a walk, or a kid wanting a snack, or a stack of student papers that need to be graded. Then the phone rings. I answer a couple of e-mails. I check Facebook. I clean the kitchen. Being a writer means making a decision that there must be downtime during my day when all of those distractions can be pushed away to make time for the story. When I don't give time to the story, it builds up inside me like a sneeze that wants to come out. I become edgy and I snap at people. Then I realize what's wrong. I have been neglecting the story. So I sit and write for a while, and I write and write. And then I can sigh and breathe.

What do you do on a rainy day?

We have an old, empty barn attached to our house, and on rainy days, the kids and I like to go in there to listen to the sound of the rain on the roof. We once spent a hurricane up there, while the windows rattled and rain lashed above us. At the top of the barn, we have comfy old couches and chairs. There is a rocking horse and a dartboard and a train table and a wooden marble run, and blocks of all sizes. I like to lie on the couch and look up at the ceiling and wonder what went on in this barn a hundred years ago. Rainy days are the perfect days for day-dreaming.

What's the best advice you have ever received about writing?

The best advice I have ever received about writing was given to me when I was in middle school. My teacher knew I wanted to be a "real writer." I wanted to be published some day, and I wanted it so badly that it almost hurt sometimes. I asked him if he thought I would become a real writer one day. I'll never forget what he said. "If you want to be a writer, you will be a writer. All you have to do is keep writing. Be patient with yourself. Never give up." He was right. It wasn't always easy, but he was right. Now, when young writers ask my advice, I give the same words to them. If I can do it, you can do it too.

Did anything from your life inspire you to write *Without Tess*?

When I was a little girl, I believed very deeply in magic. I believed that unicorns and wizards were real, and if I concentrated hard enough on a candle flame or a soap bubble or a cloud, I could move it with my mind. My favorite people in the world were other kids who knew how to play make-believe as fiercely and completely as I did. One of my very best playmates was my cousin, Jill, who was just a little bit older than I was. She had a fabulous imagination, and when I was with her, I used to feel my own magic was even stronger. If we wished hard enough, one day we could lift into the air and fly. I remember we used to draw blazes on our heads with face paint and pretend we were a team of high-stepping winged horses. We would link arms and trot all around the house, throwing back our heads and whinnying.

Jill died of cancer when we were children. It was, and still is, the saddest and most difficult thing that has ever happened in my life. When she died, I stopped wanting to think about magic. How could there be such a thing as magic or make-believe when someone so wonderful and so precious to me was no longer in the world to play with me? Even though Jill and Tess were nothing alike (thank goodness, Jill did not share Tess's struggle with mental illness), this story came from my own desire to explore what it means to mourn for a dear playmate. The story is an elegy to make-believe, an elegy to childhood, and an elegy to her. It is that sense of longing that drives the plot. How do we heal when something happens in our life that breaks us open? How do we grow up, but still keep that beautiful and heartbreaking possibility of magic alive inside of us?

What was the most difficult part of writing this novel?
The most difficult part of writing this novel was putting myself inside Lizzie's sadness. Her sense of loss, her yearning, and her guilt are all palpable and powerful forces in the story, and they were present in my life, every day while I wrote. Each time I sat down to write, I had to inhabit that space. I had to figure out ways to exist in the world with that sadness on my shoulders. I had to mourn. I would write a chapter and then take a walk and then write another chapter and then take another walk. I would cry and sing and pace around. I would sit on the dock at our summerhouse in Gloucester, Massachusetts, and look out at the water. I would watch the seagulls and the wading birds at low tide and wonder where magic goes when it dies. During the year and a half when I was working on this book, I sometimes felt as though I was being haunted by both Tess and Lizzie. They wanted their stories to be told. They pulled at my sleeves and demanded that I pay attention. I thought about them during the day, and dreamed about them at night.

The sibling dynamic is really important to this novel. Are you writing from experience, imagination, or a little of both?

Good fiction is always a mixture of experience and imagination. What happens to us when we sit down to write? Maybe we have lingering questions about our own life we want to answer. Something inspires us: a memory, a feeling, an experience. And then, when we sit down to write the inspiration down, whatever was "real" falls away. That catalyst is replaced by the narrative, which takes over like a wildflower garden and blossoms all on its own. Magic. My beloved sister, Marilyn, does not have much in common with Tess. In fact, she is kind of shy and introverted, and as a little girl, she liked to spend her time in trees reading quiet books, with her lovely bare feet curled around a branch and her head leaning back against the bark. She liked bears and fairy houses. But there are other things about Tess and Lizzie that were true about my own sister and me.

Even though the relationship between Lizzie and Tess seems unusual because of Tess's mental illness, there are lots of things about their relationship that are true between many siblings. There is jealousy. There is the desire to be close to each other, but also to be individuals. There is the desire to grow up as fast as possible, and also the desire to stay small forever, to hold onto magic and make-believe as long as we can. There is the desire to run far away from each other and also the desire to hold each other close and never ever let go. Lots of sisters experience these feelings for each other. In the end, the story of Lizzie and Tess is a story about the love between sisters and the strength of the ties that bind us together.

What do you imagine Lizzie's life to be after the end of the book?

I think at the end of the novel, there is still a lot of healing left for

Lizzie to do. She and her parents will struggle together to come to terms with what happened. They will cry and talk and hold each other. Sometimes they will become angry at each other or at themselves. Sometimes they will be silent. But little by little, they will heal and they will forgive. I like to imagine that Kaplan will always be there for Lizzie if she needs him, and maybe throughout her life, as she grows up, (especially during the times of transition when she is the most raw and vulnerable,) she will go back to visit with him to talk things through.

Kaplan's door will always be open for Lizzie, and Lizzie will always love sitting in the armchair, looking at the familiar wooden animals. Maybe she goes back to visit him just before college. And then again when she falls in love with the man she will one day marry. And then again, maybe when she is pregnant with her first child. Maybe that child will be a little girl with red hair and maybe she will give the child a name that begins with T, so that every time she calls the little girl to her side, every time she whispers her name, the first breath of sound will bring Tess back into the world for a moment.

It is amazing what people go through. We suffer tragedies. We are broken and shaken. We shatter. But then, somehow, we are able to keep on living, and eventually, we are able to see what is beautiful about the world. I think it will take a long time, but Lizzie will heal. She does not have to let go of Tess completely. She does not have to abandon creativity. She can integrate who Tess was into who she is now. She will live for both of them. Lizzie will always miss her sister. She will always have the sadness of this loss, but she is a survivor. Lizzie will never forget what if felt like to believe in magic. She will never forget what it felt like to believe she could lift into the air and fly.

★ "An expertly—and lovingly—narrated story about girls and bullying . . . Stunning."

—*Kirkus*, starred review

Turn the page for a sneak peek of

FREAK

1

REMEMBER

You do it anyway, even if it hurts,
reach back into the attic,
through the smallest opening,
and you look around in there.
I can remember some things
so clearly, I could trick myself,
imagine that I was falling
all over again. The sound of wings,
of feathered voices, whispering.

Sometimes when you try to make sense of things, they're foggy, and you have to reach way back to pull up the shadows. Even then sometimes they're too dark to really see. Other things are clear as pain, so recent that remembering takes over, and all you can do is sit back and let the memories come. When I try to write down what happened to me, this is what it's like: a symphony blaring all the parts at once, a gigantic puzzle that you have to put back together piece by piece. And all I can do is write it down fast so I only have to do it this once, and then maybe, just maybe, I'll be done with it forever.

If you asked me how the whole mess started, I would tell you it happened around the same time Artie came to stay. Artie's parents had decided to spend their sabbatical in India. They were always saying they wanted to do something good for the world, and suddenly there was this organization that was going to install hot and cold running water in a village somewhere. They asked Artie to come with them, but he wasn't about to spend his senior year digging ditches, for goodness' sake. Artie's father asked my father, and my father asked us. But before we made any decisions, we had a meeting in the living room to discuss whether or not Artie could stay. My parents call these meetings living room democracies. They're essential to our family dynamics. Each member of the family has to vote yes or no.

During living room democracies, I like to sit in the orange armchair and read the *Oxford English Dictionary*. I'm trying to memorize every word in the English language so that one day, when I become poet laureate, I can say it's because of all the words I learned when I was in seventh grade. My mom is proud of my big vocabulary. She says that when God painted me, he spent so much time making me interesting he didn't have the energy left to make me beautiful, but that's fine with her because there are more important things in life than a pretty face. I know I'm nothing like Deborah, who discovered she was beautiful when she was twelve like me. Now that she's a freshman in high school, she seems

like a flower when she walks into a room, all fragrant and bloom-
ing. It used to be that Deborah would read the *Oxford English Dictionary* with me. We'd make a pillow fort on the living room rug
and find all the Latin roots. Deborah used to say them out loud,
and I'd write them down in our notebook so we would remember
them forever.

Now, my reading the dictionary drives Deborah crazy because
it reminds her that she used to be intelligent like me. Deborah says
boys are intimidated by women who are cerebral, so I'd better
work on my Feminine Attributes, the parts that make boys turn
their heads and whistle when you walk by. Deborah has a lot of
Feminine Attributes. She wears everything low and tight so no
matter where you look, you can see skin. As for me, I like feeling
cuddled up in soft cotton. I'll choose a loose flannel shirt with the
sleeves rolled up over a skimpy little tank top any day. Mom says
it's good that I know how to be comfortable.

That evening, I was reading the *S*s all alone and I enunciated
each word toward Deborah so the sound of them spit out of my
mouth. "*Surreptitious, surreptitial, surreptitiously . . .*"

"Very nice," my father chuckled. "Now put your book away for
a minute because we have something important to talk about."

My father is what our gym teacher, Mr. Montane, calls a die-
hard liberal. Mr. Montane says this like it's a disease. Like your po-
litical beliefs can kill you. Being a die-hard liberal means not
getting cable television on purpose. It means riding a bike five
miles to Kenmore College because there are enough cars on the
road already, for goodness' sake. It means being a little shaggier
than other fathers. It means National Public Radio and chamber
music concerts and a compost heap in the backyard. I pushed the

dictionary away with my bare feet and looked at him while he talked. I like to watch his eyes twinkle.

"Okay, girls," my father said. "Your mother and I wanted to include both of you in this decision because it's going to affect us all." He looked straight at us, and I caught a glimpse of what he might be like as an English professor, talking in his soft voice, sipping on his coffee with a book of poetry in one hand. "Sid and Barbara called last night. They told us their application has been accepted. If all goes well, they'll leave for India at the end of the month. Of course they've invited Artie, but it's his senior year, and things are going so well he just doesn't want to go."

Deborah picked up the dictionary and started riffling through pages, but when she caught me watching she put it down.

"You know how important his acting career is to him," my father went on. "He has auditions for NYU in December, and the Shakespeare festival this fall. Sid asked if we would be willing to let him stay here so he could finish his senior year in peace."

"It could be healthy for us," my mother joined in, her voice smoky and tired from too many late nights in her studio trying to get ready for her opening at the Carlton Community Center. It wasn't anything special, but it was the first show she had given in years. My mother says she would have gone to art school if she hadn't had Deborah so early, but sometimes God works in mysterious ways. My mother's paintings are an acquired taste. They are filled with blurred lines and dusty colors. My mother always has paint under her fingernails and her black hair always has hints of color from her work the night before. That day she had a strand of yellow just behind her ear that made it look like she had dipped her hair in mustard.

"I was telling your father last night. It could be good to have another man around here. A little testosterone to balance the energies."

Deborah rolled her eyes. "Oh, I think he'll bring more than a little testosterone. Artie's totally girl crazy these days."

Artie didn't used to be girl crazy. When he was in middle school, he would come over to play chess with me even though I was only eight. He was pretty good at chess, but sometimes his mind would wander and he would lose track of how I was plotting my attacks. Then I'd win. Or maybe he let me win. I was never sure.

"Judy Clarke told me Artie's the hottest guy in the drama club. Even the popular girls are noticing him now," Deborah said.

"Whatever that means," sighed my mother. "The point is, Artie needs a family. We've known him his whole life. I think we should let him stay."

My father held his cup of coffee. With his other hand, he pushed a mop of hair back onto his head. I know my father is going bald, even if he'll never admit it. He's letting the curly hair on the sides of his head grow long so he can brush it over his bald spot. At first you couldn't really tell, and the extra hair just looked like misplaced bangs, but after a few years the bald in the middle got bigger and the hair on the sides got thinner.

My mother licked two of her fingers and smoothed my father's hair. She's always licking her fingers for one reason or another: either to taste a drop of spilled coffee or to twist her paintbrush into a point or to rub a smudge of dirt off my cheek. I hate it when she does that. She'll lick her fingers and then grab me by the arm so I can't get away. Then she'll rub my cheek hard with wet fingers.

There, she always says, *that's better.* There is nothing worse than having your mother's saliva on your face. Except maybe having it in your hair.

My father didn't seem to mind it, though. He stretched his bare feet on the coffee table and offered her a sip of his coffee. It was espresso. It made our living room smell like a bohemian café. My mother wrinkled her nose and waved his hand away.

"Just think of all the good times you girls had whenever we visited Artie's house," my father said. "Think of all the dinners and slide shows."

"And all the memories of Thanksgiving," my mother sighed. Her voice always sounds like it's sighing. All her sentences dip down at the end like they are falling slowly down rabbit holes, trailing away. "Think of that wonderful Thanksgiving a few years ago. Can you remember it, girls? All those candied yams."

I remembered one Thanksgiving, but not because of the candied yams. We were all in elementary school, and Artie showed us real dead monkey skulls and told us this was how we looked on the inside. Deborah thought it was inhumane to dissect monkeys, and I did too. But the dead monkey skulls had jaws that opened and closed. While everyone was eating apple pie, Artie and I brought a couple of skulls to the dinner table and popped them out in front of Deborah while she was chewing. Opening and closing the jaws, we made them say *monkey see, monkey do* . . . until Deborah threw down her fork and marched off, announcing, *Don't be disgusting.* It was wonderful.

"I don't care as long as he doesn't take a long time in the shower or walk around nude," Deborah announced from the carved rocking chair.

ing chair so that she was balanced on its wooden tips and I could see down her shirt to her lacy pink bra. The rocking chair creaked under her weight.

I reached over the table and grabbed my father's espresso with both hands. The smell was so strong I almost dropped it onto the rug, but I closed my eyes tight and, taking a deep breath, downed the whole thing.

"Yes!" I cried. "Yes, I think he should definitely stay here!"

"You are such an alien," Deborah said, rolling her eyes.

I picked up the *National Geographic* and pretended to read, but inside, my heart was pounding. Artie Rosenberg was going to move into our house. Artie with his monkey skulls, Artie with his rehearsals and his scripts, Artie with his yellow Volkswagen Bug and his books of poetry, Artie who knew how to swear in Arabic! Artie Rosenberg, in our house, for a whole year. I turned the page of the *National Geographic*. There was a Pygmy man, standing with a spear in his hand. And he wasn't wearing anything. Not even a loincloth.

Judging from the length of her showers since she started school, it was hard to imagine that anyone could take longer Deborah. I started to think of what Artie might look like in nude, but that made me blush. I picked up a *National Geograp* and flipped through the pages. I stopped for color pictures of Py mies in skimpy loincloths. I didn't want to contribute to the famil meeting. I couldn't possibly be part of this living room democracy. The thought of Artie living in our house for a whole year was too horrible—and too wonderful—to imagine. He was the only high school senior I had ever known.

Artie was old enough to shave and drive a car, and he knew the names of all the *Star Trek* episodes. He could recite Shakespeare with a real British accent. And best of all, he loved poetry. He had books and books of poetry on his bedroom bookshelf. One time when I was a little girl, he let me look at his collection of Dylan Thomas. I sat on his floor for hours and memorized the poems until Mom called and made me come home. *Apple boughs. Lilting house. Dingle starry. Heydays of his eyes.* I still remember how it felt to say those wonderful, delicious words.

"What do you think, Miriam?" my mother asked.

"What?" I looked up from the *National Geographic.*

"What do you think about Artie coming to stay with us for a while?"

My mother and father leaned forward and waited for me to speak.

"I don't care," I said.

"We all have to vote," Deborah told me, her voice irritating and superior. "If we don't all vote then it's only a partial democracy, and any decision is null and void." She leaned forward on the rock-

Judging from the length of her showers since she started high school, it was hard to imagine that anyone could take longer than Deborah. I started to think of what Artie might look like in the nude, but that made me blush. I picked up a *National Geographic* and flipped through the pages. I stopped for color pictures of Pygmies in skimpy loincloths. I didn't want to contribute to the family meeting. I couldn't possibly be part of this living room democracy. The thought of Artie living in our house for a whole year was too horrible—and too wonderful—to imagine. He was the only high school senior I had ever known.

Artie was old enough to shave and drive a car, and he knew the names of all the *Star Trek* episodes. He could recite Shakespeare with a real British accent. And best of all, he loved poetry. He had books and books of poetry on his bedroom bookshelf. One time when I was a little girl, he let me look at his collection of Dylan Thomas. I sat on his floor for hours and memorized the poems until Mom called and made me come home. *Apple boughs. Lilting house. Dingle starry. Heydays of his eyes.* I still remember how it felt to say those wonderful, delicious words.

"What do you think, Miriam?" my mother asked.

"What?" I looked up from the *National Geographic.*

"What do you think about Artie coming to stay with us for a while?"

My mother and father leaned forward and waited for me to speak.

"I don't care," I said.

"We all have to vote," Deborah told me, her voice irritating and superior. "If we don't all vote then it's only a partial democracy, and any decision is null and void." She leaned forward on the rocking chair so that she was balanced on its wooden tips and I could see down her shirt to her lacy pink bra. The rocking chair creaked under her weight.

I reached over the table and grabbed my father's espresso with both hands. The smell was so strong I almost dropped it onto the rug, but I closed my eyes tight and, taking a deep breath, downed the whole thing.

"Yes!" I cried. "Yes, I think he should definitely stay here!"

"You are such an alien," Deborah said, rolling her eyes.

I picked up the *National Geographic* and pretended to read, but inside, my heart was pounding. Artie Rosenberg was going to move into our house. Artie with his monkey skulls, Artie with his rehearsals and his scripts, Artie with his yellow Volkswagen Bug and his books of poetry, Artie who knew how to swear in Arabic! Artie Rosenberg, in our house, for a whole year. I turned the page of the *National Geographic*. There was a Pygmy man, standing with a spear in his hand. And he wasn't wearing anything. Not even a loincloth.